Getting the job at the Too Chic Boutique was the least of my problems. Sure, Libby's out to sabotage me. But Tanya's the one I really have to worry about. You see, Cousin Tanya will do anything to prove her magic is stronger than mine. She jinxed my first day at the store. Then she turned my cat, Salem, into a stuffed pink toy . . . and transformed me into an old hag! My Black Book doesn't say *anything* about witch vs. witch. Salem won't talk (for a change!) and my aunts say self-defense is one lesson nobody can teach me. What's a witch to do? But I'm getting ahead of myself.

My name's Sabrina and I'm sixteen. I always knew I was different, but I thought it was just because I lived with my strange aunts, Zelda and Hilda, while my divorced parents bounced around the world. Dad's in the foreign service. The *very* foreign service. He's a witch—and so am I.

I can't run to Mom—but *not* because she's currently on an archaeological dig in Peru. She's a mortal. If I set eyes on her in the next two years, she'll turn into a ball of wax. So for now, I'm stuck with my aunts. They're hanging around to show me everything I need to know about this witch business. They say all I have to do is concentrate and point. And I thought fitting in was tough!

You probably think I have superpowers. Think again! I can't turn back time and I'm on my own when it comes to love. Of course, there are some pretty neat things I *can* do—but that's where the trouble *always* begins. . . .

Sabrina, the Teenage Witch™ books

#1 Sabrina, the Teenage Witch
#2 Showdown at the Mall

Available from ARCHWAY Paperbacks

Sabrina The Teenage Witch™

Showdown at the Mall

Diana G. Gallagher

AN ARCHWAY PAPERBACK
Published by POCKET BOOKS
New York London Toronto Sydney Tokyo Singapore

This book is a work of fiction. Names, characters, places and incidents are products of the author's imagination or are used fictitiously. Any resemblance to actual events or locales or persons, living or dead, is entirely coincidental.

AN ARCHWAY PAPERBACK *Original*

An Archway Paperback published by
POCKET BOOKS, a division of Simon & Schuster Inc.
1230 Avenue of the Americas, New York, NY 10020

ISBN: 0-671-01434-X

First Archway Paperback printing June 1997

10 9 8 7 6 5 4 3 2 1

Cover photo by Don Cadette

Printed in the U.S.A.

IL 5+

For Sharon Middleton,
a longtime friend and fan
whose support is greatly appreciated

Showdown at the Mall

Chapter 1

☆

"What do you think, Sabrina?" Jenny Kelly whispered, keeping a wary eye on Mr. Pool as she leaned closer.

Sabrina glanced at her best friend and shrugged. "Sounds like it might be fun."

"Spending a whole weekend working?" Jenny asked, raising a skeptical eyebrow. A mass of wavy light brown hair cascaded over her shoulders and a shadow of doubt clouded her eyes.

"Depends on *where* we're working, doesn't it?"

"Yeah. I guess it does." Nodding, Jenny sat back with a heavy sigh. "I'll probably get stuck selling kids' shoes or something."

"The Big Cookie would be cool." Harvey Kinkle glanced back with a mischievous grin, then frowned suddenly. "But I'd probably have to pay for what I eat, huh?"

Nodding, Sabrina smiled as Harvey absently brushed a renegade lock of sandy brown hair off his forehead. Harvey was totally charming and gorgeous and didn't know it, which just made him more charming and gorgeous. And he liked her as much as she liked him. There had been no chase, no coy game playing or determined effort to "catch" each other. Over the months, a mutual bond of affection had been forged based on friendship. And Jenny wasn't the least bit upset or jealous, even though she had once been interested in Harvey, too. On the other hand, Libby Chessler refused to accept defeat with a vengeance and persisted in trying to drive a wedge between them. Without success. Except for the cheerleader, the proverbial and apparently permanent thorn in her side, Sabrina's life was on a fast track to perfect.

Tearing her gaze away from Harvey, Sabrina focused on the science teacher as he finished explaining the Teen Work Weekend project being sponsored by the mall.

"You'll be paid, of course." Mr. Pool waited until a smattering of applause and whistles died down. "Minimum wage." He paused again as almost everyone groaned. "But money isn't why you'll be participating."

"It's why *I* am!" a deep voice bellowed from the back.

"I didn't know we had a choice." Pouting, Laura Thomas, a thin girl who wore glasses because contacts made her eyes water, dropped her chin on her hand.

"You don't." Mr. Pool stopped pacing. "Look at it as a crash course in real life, a no-risk opportunity to go out and tackle the business world." Noting the excessive number of blank faces staring back at him, the teacher shifted his gaze toward the classroom door, then bent forward slightly and lowered his voice. "A chance to spend two whole days at the mall!"

"Too fab!" Darlene Maroney giggled, then frowned as she noticed her nail enamel had chipped.

"I'd rather go to the library." Jerry Evans, a husky boy with freckles and a brain that rivaled Einstein's, slumped in his seat. He was determined to win a Nobel prize for physics by the age of thirty and resented anything that interfered with the pursuit of his goal.

"What do you mean by 'no-risk'?" Libby stood up, drawing all eyes to the green and white cheerleader's outfit she flaunted with a self-assured arrogance. With her long, shining, dark hair, a touch of makeup, and direct, unruffled demeanor, Libby proclaimed her elevated high school status without uttering a single word.

And everyone got the message loud and clear.

Glancing back, Sabrina smothered a frustrated sigh with her hand. She didn't understand how someone as conceited and overbearing as Libby had become the most popular girl in school. Being pretty, pushy, and totally poised probably had a lot to do with it. Still, nobody except her best friends Jill and Cee Cee actually seemed to *like* Libby, but apparently, being nice wasn't a factor on the popularity scale. Power was. And Libby had power, which she wielded with a disdain for the student body masses that would have made the most ruthless of Europe's past monarchs proud.

"No-risk because getting the job you're assigned is pretty much guaranteed," Mr. Pool said. "Although if anyone *really* botches his interview this afternoon, his prospective employer has the option to just forget it."

"If we've already got the jobs, why do we have to interview?" Libby sat down, her challenging gaze fixed on Mr. Pool.

"So you can experience what a job interview is like. That's the whole point of this project. Experience." Mr. Pool's eyes narrowed as a redheaded boy crossed his eyes and held his arms out at an awkward angle. The teacher smiled at him. "And don't think you can deliberately screw up and get this weekend off. I'll hear about it and I've got enough yard and housework to keep all of you busy for two days."

An epidemic of rolling eyes swept through the room.

Sabrina shifted toward Jenny as Mr. Pool began filling a goldfish bowl with folded pieces of paper. "Where do you want to work?"

"Anywhere but kids' shoes. I don't think I could deal with stuffing tiny curled toes into tight new shoes for two days without going mad. I'm not crazy about tropical fish, either. What about you?"

"No question." Sabrina crossed her fingers. "Too Chic Boutique."

"With your plebeian sense of style?" Behind her, Libby scoffed. Her contemptuous gaze flicked over Sabrina's short-sleeved, rose-colored pullover and belted jeans. "Fashion is *not* exactly your forte, Sabrina."

Sabrina smiled tightly. "At least I don't wear a *uniform* half the time." She quickly turned away as Mr. Pool held up the goldfish bowl.

"Too Chic Boutique is *mine!*" Libby hissed.

"Who's first?" The science teacher's enthusiastic smile faded as he looked around the room. Twenty-five faces with expressions ranging from totally bored to totally terrified stared back. No one raised a hand. "Aw, come on, guys. You're not being condemned to hard labor on a road gang. You might even enjoy yourselves."

No one moved.

Sabrina hesitated, not from reluctance to work or fear, but because she couldn't decide *when* her chances of picking the "in" clothing store would be better. At the moment, the odds were twenty-five to one, but if she waited too long, someone else might pick that paper first.

Mr. Pool didn't see Libby raise her hand as he wandered up the aisle. He stopped by Jenny and held out the bowl.

Closing her eyes, Jenny slowly drew out a paper. She took a deep breath before reading it, then heaved an exaggerated sigh of relief. "The Dickens Den."

Sabrina gave her a thumbs-up and reached to dip into the bowl. The odds were long, but at least the paper with Too Chic Boutique was still up for grabs. Now was as good a time as any.

"I'll go next, Mr. Pool!" Libby waved her hand.

"Sure." The teacher pulled the bowl out from under Sabrina's outstretched hand with an apologetic shrug. "Libby wrote out the slips for me. It's only fair."

"No problem." Sabrina sat back, then tensed as the cheerleader impaled her with a look of smug confidence. Libby had taken an immediate dislike to her when she started attending Westbridge High. The only thing that had saved Sabrina from feeling like a hopelessly clumsy social pariah was finding out that she was a witch with some awesome powers of her own. A special dispensation from the Witch's Council had turned back time, allowing her to relive that horrible first day so she could fix everything that had gone wrong. Since then, a combination of wits and witchcraft had prevented Libby from making her life miserable.

But nothing had stopped Libby from trying.

Suddenly suspicious, Sabrina watched closely as Libby put her hand in the bowl. The cheerleader didn't close or avert her eyes. A frown of concentration knit her brow as her fingers sifted through the folded slips, causing some of them to open slightly. Sabrina noticed Libby's triumphant smile and the obvious black slash on an inner corner of a paper in the same instant.

Libby had marked the slip for the Too Chic Boutique.

And Sabrina was not about to let her get away with it.

As Libby's hand closed around the marked paper, Sabrina casually pointed at the bowl. Her fingertip tingled as she released a small but effective surge of witch's magic. A different folded paper zipped into Libby's hand as the marked paper slipped out. Libby was totally unaware of the switch. Although tempted to take advantage of the other girl's effort to cheat, Sabrina decided to play fair. She had learned the hard way that using magic for personal gain had an infuriating tendency to backfire. As soon as the cheerleader's hand was clear of the bowl, she pointed again, erasing the telltale black slash with a flick of her finger. She'd take her chances along with everyone else.

"Aren't you going to open it?" Mr. Pool asked as Libby relaxed with the paper clutched in her fist.

"Not just yet." Libby graced Sabrina with another smug smile. Following her lead, Jill and Cee Cee drew out papers and held on to them without looking, too.

Then the bowl was in front of Sabrina again. Breathing deeply, she reached in and drew. With a casual glance at the folded paper, she placed it on her desk and leaned back.

"You're not going to look, either?" Jenny asked.

"No, I'll wait." Sabrina didn't have a clue where she would end up working this weekend. But if she had lucked out and drawn Too Chic Boutique, she didn't want Libby to know. Not just yet. She wanted to savor the anticipation of watching Libby open her own slip only to discover she had not gotten the job she wanted.

Choosing students at random, Mr. Pool moved between desks with the bowl. The novelty store, health foods, computer software, and one of three CD music stores were drawn and met with varying degrees of disgust and delight.

"The Sports Palace." Harvey nodded, graciously accepting the luck of the draw as he did just about everything that life tossed his way. "That's almost as good as cookies. I won't have to bake anything, but I might get awfully hungry."

"Don't worry about your stomach," Sabrina assured him. "We'll meet for lunch in the Food Court. You, too, Jenny."

"Excellent! I've always wanted to 'do lunch.'" Jenny beamed. "And the bookstore shouldn't be too bad. I mean, how hard can that be? You ask someone what they like and steer them to the right shelves. And if business is slow, I can browse through the latest magazines."

"How come you're not opening yours?" Harvey asked.

Sabrina shrugged. "Because chances are I didn't get what I really want. But as long as I don't know for sure, there's still a chance. See?"

"No." Harvey blinked, totally bewildered.

"Exactly." Jenny nodded with understanding.

When all the slips had been distributed and the places of temporary employment revealed, everyone turned to stare at the four girls who had not read their papers.

One of them had Too Chic Boutique.

The suspense mounted as Jill and then Cee Cee opened their papers and sagged. Sabrina stifled an excited squeal as they mumbled the names of Country Crafts and Gourmet Wares. The trendy, totally cool fashion store was hers!

But Libby still thought she had bagged the prized assignment.

Maintaining an expression of anxious curiosity, Sabrina met the composed gaze that betrayed Libby's certainty as she unfolded the paper. The cheerleader's mouth twitched and started to curl into a smile as she glanced at the paper.

"Toy Town—" Libby blinked with a gasp of horrified disbelief. "Hobbies and games? But—there must be some mistake!"

Sabrina quickly opened her own slip and held it up. "No mistake! I've got Too Chic Boutique!"

Laughing out loud, Jenny shook Sabrina's arm. "Way!"

"Cool." Harvey winked.

Maybe, Sabrina thought as Libby leaned over and snatched the paper from her hand.

"Let me see that!" The cheerleader's eyes narrowed when she realized the black mark was gone. She couldn't accuse Sabrina of cheating because the evidence had mysteriously vanished. Nor could she admit that she had marked the slip in the first place. Still, even though there was no logical explanation, she suspected Sabrina had done *something* to ruin her carefully prepared plan to snag the boutique for herself.

As Mr. Pool returned to the front of the room, Libby shot Sabrina a withering look. "I will get you for this. Believe me."

Sabrina sighed. She had picked Too Chic Boutique fair and square, but that obviously didn't matter to the enraged girl hovering behind her. There was no way Libby could "get" her. Her magical abilities would see to that when and if it became necessary. It was just lucky for the vindictive, self-centered cheerleader that her designated rival wasn't as vindictive and power-mad as she was. Sabrina didn't go looking for trouble and she tried not to use her powers irresponsibly, but dealing with Libby's constant harassment was tedious and annoying.

And every now and then Sabrina was tempted to try solving the problem once and for all. She didn't, because using magic for evil purposes had a way of producing unexpected and unwelcome consequences.

And she had to live with herself.

Besides, turning Libby into a geek hadn't been the satisfying victory Sabrina had anticipated. Libby would probably figure out how to turn being a toad into an advantage, too.

☆

Chapter 2

☆

"The Slicery at eight?" Sabrina shifted her gaze between Harvey and Jenny, then shifted her crocheted bag to her other shoulder. It felt heavy and awkward, but at least she wasn't hauling an armload of books around the mall. None of their teachers had assigned weekend homework because of the employment project.

"I'll be there," Harvey said. "Gotta go now, though, or I'll be late for my interview." Dodging women with babies in strollers and clusters of junior-high teens, he jogged down the main concourse toward The Sports Palace.

"Are you nervous?" Jenny tugged on her multicolored paisley vest and smoothed her short skirt. "Do I look okay?"

"You look fine," Sabrina assured her, wishing

she had worn something more sophisticated to school. Jeans and a V-necked tee hardly seemed appropriate for a job interview at the most stylish clothing store in town, but there hadn't been time to go home and change. And a fast fashion adjustment in the school restroom hadn't been possible, either. Apprehensive about her interview and wanting moral support, Jenny had insisted that they go to the mall together. No way could Sabrina have explained leaving school wearing different clothes.

"Well, guess I might as well get this over with." Taking several slow, deep breaths, Jenny turned toward the bookstore and called back over her shoulder, "I'll meet you back here as soon as I'm done! Wish me luck."

"Luck!" Sabrina watched until Jenny disappeared into The Dickens Den, then checked the time. Three minutes to four. She couldn't even dash into the mall restroom and "wish" up an outfit that was more stunningly suitable, not if she wanted to make her interview on time. The ladies' lounge was off the Food Court on the second level, and the mall was too crowded to simply *pop* out and back in again.

A quick survey of the plaza under the mall's high center dome vetoed any notion Sabrina had of pulling off a Superman quick-change in a convenient concealed nook. There wasn't any place to duck into where an abrupt and dramatic change of clothes wouldn't be noticed by someone passing by. The plaza and crisscrossing concourses swarmed with Friday afternoon shoppers. Even the stone benches under the overhanging limbs of impeccably trimmed, potted trees were full. Elderly couples rubbed aching feet. Young mothers frantically hushed squalling toddlers, and teenagers congregated for no discernible purpose except to hang somewhere where something interesting *might* happen.

Sitting near the towering central fountain, a young woman with long dark hair and an exquisitely beautiful face caught Sabrina's eye. Wearing flowing wide-legged pants and a matching blue-gray jacket complemented by a long-sleeved white blouse with a tapered collar, she alternately looked at her watch or stared into space with an expression of absolute boredom. Remote in attitude and elegant in feature, the unfamiliar girl had a high-fashion look and presence that made Sabrina feel style-challenged.

Two minutes and counting.

Sabrina sighed. She had only two options: skip the interview and spend the weekend weeding Mr. Pool's marigolds, or go for it.

No contest.

Running a comb through her shoulder-length blond hair, Sabrina turned to face Too Chic Boutique. Reminding herself that she was just going through the motions of interviewing for a job that was already hers, she strode forward with an outward appearance of calm confidence that belied the churning in her stomach. Being cool and chic was a matter of attitude—not attire.

As she approached the open doorway beyond an arched alcove, the tall, slim mannequins in the store's side windows seemed to mock her with permanently somber expressions of scornful superiority. Draped in dark brown, sky blue, and apple green ensembles ranging from casual vests and slacks to sleek sequined evening wear, the sculpted guardians of style silently dared the dowdy and desperate to enter.

"Smile!" With a flick of her finger Sabrina altered the face and posture of the nearest molded figure. Plastic arms jerked, then bent at odd angles as the mannequin slumped forward to stare at the floor with crossed eyes and a lopsided grin. The low-cut neckline of its fitted jacket flopped open, destroying any essence of grace the designer had hoped to achieve.

Mr. Pool had given her the manager's name and a brief description. The woman with short-clipped red hair standing behind a curved counter had to be Aubrey Holcomb. *Attitude is everything.* Sabrina held on to that thought as she swept through the store.

"Ms. Holcomb?"

"Yes." The tall, willowy woman stepped into the aisle with flowing, feline grace and fixed Sabrina with startling green eyes.

And she's *got enough attitude for both of us.*

Wearing a fitted forest green pants suit with a soft cowl-necked shirt, she bore a disquieting resemblance to the grim mannequins in the windows. Every wisp of combed-back hair was in place. Her manicured nails gleamed with an unmarred coral luster and her makeup was sparingly applied with professional expertise. Not a single wrinkle dared crease the fabric of her outfit or her flawless face. Smiling tightly, she gave Sabrina a brisk, unimpressed once-over.

"And how may I help you?"

Refusing to be intimidated, Sabrina countered with a brighter smile and held out her hand. "Actually, I'm here to help you, Ms. Holcomb. Sabrina Spellman. I've been assigned to your store for the Teen Work Weekend project."

"I see." The woman's eyes narrowed with unguarded dismay. "Do you have any experience?"

"Uh, no—" Sabrina hesitated as the manager sighed, folded her arms, scrutinized her with a critical eye, and then shook her head slightly. Assuming the woman was concerned about her too-casual clothes, she hastened to explain. "I didn't know I'd be going on a job interview when I dressed this morning. If I had, I wouldn't have worn jeans—"

"The fit is all wrong," Aubrey said bluntly.

"But they're comfortable!" Wiping a self-conscious smile off her face, Sabrina cleared her throat. She wasn't sure what she had expected the interview to be like, but she certainly hadn't expected to be subjected to an appraisal based on whether or not her jeans fit in accordance with the manager's standards of style.

"Such an obvious department-store look won't work here, I'm afraid. Too Chic Boutique has an image that must be maintained—without exception. Sorry."

"Sorry?" Sabrina stared at her. "That's it?"

"What else is there?" Aubrey asked.

How about a zit in the middle of your forehead or a severe case of permanent pucker lips? Sabrina fumed, but she kept her temper and her finger in check.

Libby stood on the edge of the central plaza, staring at Too Chic Boutique. "I can't believe that shabby Sabrina Spellman got my job! Just *look* at her!"

Several people turned to stare as Libby shrieked her outrage. Except for one impeccably dressed girl sitting close by, she forced all of them to avert their curious eyes with the power of her own furious glance.

Flanking their inconsolable leader, Jill and Cee Cee peered through the windows of the fashion shop and nodded.

"It's definitely not fair, Libby," Cee Cee said.

"Sabrina is so—so—" Jill shrugged, at a loss for the right word.

"Pedestrian." Libby's unhappy scowl darkened as she spat out the invective. She had breezed through her interview at Toy Town, even though it had been more of a nightmare than she had thought possible. Rodney Snivitz was a college geek with disgusting acne and thick glasses who thought he was hot stuff just because he was the manager. Only the thought of having to wash Mr. Pool's dirty clothes had induced Libby to turn on the charm. Snivitz had been defenseless against her. Charm, however, had absolutely no effect on eight-year-olds determined to test drive every pedaled or battery-powered vehicle in the store. And collision insurance wasn't included in her employee benefits. Libby rubbed the bruise on her shin, painfully aware that the reddish-purple blotch was swelling to the size of a halved baseball.

"Definitely not fair," Cee Cee repeated. "Too bad there isn't something we can do."

"Maybe there is," Libby said with a sly grin. "If Sabrina botches the interview, she won't get the job. And if she doesn't get it, there's nothing to stop me from stepping in to take her place."

"What if she doesn't botch the interview?" Jill asked.

"She will. Sabrina is about to prove that she couldn't sell a towel to a naked man in the middle of a busy street." Annoyed that she hadn't thought of sabotaging Sabrina's interview sooner, Libby marched toward the entrance of

Too Chic Boutique with Cee Cee and Jill following in her determined wake.

"You want to audition?" Aubrey's eyes widened ever so slightly. "For a weekend job?"

"Sure. Why not?" Unslinging her shoulder bag, Sabrina dropped it behind the curved counter. "If I sell someone something in the next fifteen minutes, the job's mine."

Aubrey pursed her full, lightly blushed lips, then shrugged. "Fair enough. Your first customer just walked through the door."

"Great! Thanks, Ms. Holcomb. You won't be sorry!" Beaming, Sabrina turned to greet her ticket to the ranks of Too Chic Boutique employ, and inhaled sharply.

Libby?

Was this part of a cosmic conspiracy to punish her for preventing the cheerleader from getting the store, or what? Sabrina immediately dismissed that possibility. True, she had used magic to keep Libby from cheating to get Too Chic, but she hadn't used her powers to get the job for herself. Libby's untimely arrival with her everpresent entourage was simply an unfortunate coincidence.

And she was stuck with it.

"Hi, Libby!" Smiling, Sabrina strolled over to the three girls as they paused to browse through a rack of mix-and-match vests, short skirts, and flared pants. "Jill. Cee Cee. How'd your interviews go?"

"Like *you're* really interested." Rolling her eyes, Jill turned away to flip absently through the pastel-colored tees on a circular rack.

Dropping the subject, Sabrina picked out a smoke blue vest with a delicate pattern embroidered in gold on the front panels. Holding it up in front of Libby, she stood back to study the effect. "This is a great shade for your coloring. It brings out the highlights in your hair."

"I hate blue." Eyes flashing, Libby snatched the hanger out of her hand and tossed the vest aside.

Sabrina blinked. "You wear blue all the time, Libby."

"But not today!"

Out of the corner of her eye, Sabrina saw the stunning girl from the plaza saunter into the store. Suspecting that Libby had only come in to give her a hard time, she excused herself when the other girl pointed in her direction, unobtrusively, but obviously asking for assistance. *Definitely a better prospect for a sale,* Sabrina thought as she stepped backward, bumping into Jill.

"Watch it!" Jill sidestepped, pushing Sabrina away.

Thrown off balance, Sabrina stumbled into the rack of T-shirts. Hangers clattered on the metal bar as the rack began to topple. Righting herself, she managed to keep the rack from falling over, but stepped on Cee Cee's foot.

"Ouch!" Cee Cee glared at Sabrina. "You are such a spaz sometimes!"

"So-so-sorry. I, uh—uh, do-don't know what hap-happened!" Flustered, Sabrina clamped her mouth shut. What was going on? She wasn't clumsy and she didn't stutter! Not usually.

"I'll try these on." With a satisfied smirk, Libby tore three vests, a skirt, and two pairs of pants off the rack and stuffed them into Sabrina's arms. "And this and this!" She yanked two tees off the rack behind her and tossed them onto the pile.

"And I'll try these!" Jill added two more tees and a skirt to the load.

Staggering under several layers of fabric, Sabrina wondered if she was allergic to something she had eaten, something that had no adverse effect on mortals but turned witches into bumbling, stammering dimwits! Maybe, but figuring out *why* she had suddenly developed an acute dysfunction of coordination wasn't nearly as urgent as fixing it. Shifting the stack of clothes into one arm, she pointed to herself and concentrated.

In control, calm, and cool, she silently intoned. *No more the babbling, clumsy fool.*

"Ri-right th-th-this way!" Sabrina stuttered as she turned to locate the fitting room. Astounded by the failure of the spell to cure her unexplained speech impediment, she didn't realize the stack of clothes was slipping off her arm, until it was too late. Clutching and grasping, she sank to her knees as she tried to hang on to them. Her fumbling only made the situation worse as clothes and hangers tumbled into a heap of tangled color on the polished floor. *This is not happening!* Scrambling to gather the outfits back into her arms, Sabrina valiantly struggled back to her feet. All she could do was forge ahead, hoping whatever strange malady she had contracted would go away as fast as it had struck.

"Th-the fi-fi-fitting room's o-over—"

"Forget it, Sabrina," Libby interrupted loudly. "I'm not trying on clothes you've used to mop the floor!"

Watching from the counter, Aubrey Holcomb sighed and shook her head.

"Me neither," Jill said with an emphatic nod.

"Bu—but—but—" Sabrina stared, bewildered and devastated as Libby and her friends brushed past her. When Libby made an abrupt detour toward the curved counter and the stricken manager, Sabrina rushed forward to intercept, stumbled over her own feet, and went sprawling on the floor. The pile of clothes she clutched to her chest saved her from incurring any bumps or bruises, but nothing could save her wounded pride and dignity.

"My condolences, Ms. Holcomb." Libby's voice dripped with feigned sincerity. "Sabrina tries hard, but—well, some people just can't get it together under pressure. However, as I understand it, you don't have to hire anyone who's unsuitable just because they pulled the name of your store out of a fishbowl."

Aubrey raised an interested eyebrow as Libby took a business card from the holder on the counter and wrote on the back. She glanced at Sabrina and smiled as she handed it to the manager. "Here's my number."

Angry and upset, Sabrina rose to her feet with the wrinkled clothes still crushed in her arms. Libby rushed past on her way to the door, where Jill and Cee Cee were waiting. She didn't stop to gloat. There would be plenty of time for that later, Sabrina realized, when they were back in school on Monday. Then Libby would be able to savor the effects of completely humiliating her in front of everyone when she announced Sabrina hadn't gotten the choice job after all, but had spent the weekend scrubbing Mr. Pool's kitchen floor and washing his windows.

For a moment, Sabrina thought she might still have a fighting chance. The fashionable, unfamiliar girl in blue was watching her. The girl motioned with her hand, then apparently thought better of calling Sabrina over. Averting her gaze, she turned and followed the cheerleaders out of the store.

"I'm sorry, Sabrina—"

Sabrina jumped as Aubrey came up behind her.

"But Too Chic Boutique can't afford having you in the store for a whole weekend. It would take months to recover from the loss of business"—Aubrey's gaze flicked toward the four girls retreating into the mall. Then, wrinkling her nose, she liberated one of the hangers from Sabrina's grasp and held it at arm's length—"and merchandise."

Sabrina nodded in defeat as she studied the gold-embroidered, magnolia pink vest dangling before her. There was no way to argue with the limp and rumpled evidence of her inept bumbling.

She just hoped she wouldn't have to wash, tumble-dry, and fold Mr. Pool's socks and underwear.

Chapter 3

Then again, when have I ever given up easily?

Sabrina considered that for all of a nanosecond.

Never. Especially when she wanted something as badly as she wanted the job at Too Chic Boutique.

Aubrey suddenly looked toward the door and frowned.

Sabrina took advantage of the moment to try another spell. Maybe her previous magic malfunction had been temporary, a side effect of her unexplained loss of equilibrium. With a quick wag of her finger, the wrinkled, dust-covered vest was pressed and clean. She almost giggled with relief, but contained herself.

"Jocelyn, Jocelyn . . ." Aubrey muttered

softly. Exhaling with weary exasperation, she handed the vest back to Sabrina without looking at it. "Why today? Haven't I been through enough?"

"Who's Jocelyn?" Aubrey's head snapped around to look at her curiously, and Sabrina suddenly realized that the mysterious stutter was gone. She listened as she sorted the clothes she was holding and hung them on an empty rack.

"Jocelyn Harrington has an unlimited allowance, compliments of her wealthy father, and the figure of a . . . well, let's just say she will spend hours trying on hot new styles she can't possibly wear and leave buying nothing, swearing never to return. Unfortunately, she always does. And I despise waiting on her. It's just so—pathetic."

"My time's not up yet." With nothing to lose and everything to gain, Sabrina eagerly volunteered. "I mean, if Jocelyn's as difficult to please as you say, there's not much chance I'll sell her anything and you'll be off the hook to hire me."

Aubrey started, thought a moment, then almost smiled. "An excellent idea. After she's spent a few minutes with you, maybe she'll keep her word and never come back."

"But if she buys something, I've got the job." Hanging up the last vest, Sabrina flicked her finger toward the rack, giving the creased clothes a quick clean-and-press. "A deal's a deal, right?"

"Of course." Certain she was soon to be rid of

both problem girls, Aubrey nodded. As Sabrina started down the aisle toward Jocelyn, the manager peered at the immaculate clothes with a puzzled frown. "Must be some kind of new miracle fabric. . . ."

"Hi! Can I help you?" Sabrina kept smiling when the short girl turned to regard her with a sneer.

"I doubt it," Jocelyn snapped. A large mole twitched just above the corner of her thin pouting mouth. Her brown eyes appeared squinty and small in the broad expanse of her round face and a too-tightly permed crown of brown curls produced an odd mushroom effect. "I never find anything in this store I like."

"I have a feeling today will be quite different."

"Why should today be any different?" The girl's tone was caustically sarcastic, but her brown eyes betrayed a curious interest.

"Because I have a knack for finding exactly the right thing for everyone." Sabrina sifted through a rack of velour tunic tops and pulled out one in sea-foam green. "This is perfect for you. Especially if you coordinate it with those." Turning abruptly, Sabrina moved down the aisle to get a pair of dark green pants made of a tight stretch-knit fabric. "Come on. The fitting room's over here."

Frowning uncertainly, but too intrigued and hopeful to resist, Jocelyn followed Sabrina across the store. She hesitated as Sabrina parted the curtain into one of the cubicles and handed her the outfit.

"These are stretch pants." Jocelyn's eyes flashed defensively. "Maybe you didn't notice, but I'm not exactly built for stretch pants."

Sabrina smiled with warm encouragement. "Everyone has some kind of figure flaw. The trick is to find clothes that don't accent them. This fabric has an absolutely phenomenal way of compacting . . . things. Trust me."

"Can't hurt, I guess." Sighing, Jocelyn stepped inside and drew the curtain closed.

Sabrina stepped back into the store to implement the next phase of her sales plan. Pointing at a full-length wall mirror, she wove another spell in a hushed whisper.

"Mirror now enchanted glass, reflect the image told her. Sleek and chic, no lumpy—" Sabrina winced, hoping one missing rhyme wouldn't matter. "—backside in the eye of the beholder." Pleased, Sabrina looked back at Aubrey.

The manager held up seven fingers.

Seven minutes. Long enough.

Dashing in the door, Jenny paused, spotted Sabrina, and started to walk over. Sabrina waved her back as Jocelyn waddled out of the fitting room.

"They're so tight!" Grimacing, the girl tried to tug on the snug-fitting pants but couldn't get a grip.

Aubrey dropped her face into her hand, as though the sight of Jocelyn stuffed into two-toned green was a painful assault on her aesthetic senses.

Jenny blinked and smothered a gasp with her hand.

"But they look great!" Sabrina lied, but it was an act of kindness. The sea-foam green top wrinkled around Jocelyn's abundant chest, arms, and midsection. Jammed into the elastic green pants, she looked like a pickled sausage. But Jocelyn didn't have to know that. Taking the girl's chubby arm, Sabrina dragged her in front of the mirror.

"I can't look." Jocelyn covered her tightly shut eyes with her pudgy hands.

Aubrey held up five fingers.

"I think you'll be pleased," Sabrina coaxed, grunting as she pried the girl's hands away from her face.

Jocelyn's huge chest heaved with a resigned sigh. Her beady eyes opened, blinked, then widened in sheer, unabashed joy as she stared into the lying mirror. "Oh, my. Oh, gosh, that can't be me! Is that me?"

Sabrina nodded, then ducked, avoiding a serious blow to the head as Jocelyn flung out her arms and twirled in front of the enchanted glass. She couldn't see what Jocelyn was seeing, but the reflected false image was obviously having the desired effect.

Three fingers.

"I'll take them! But I think I'll wear them home, if that's all right."

"Of course." As Jocelyn dashed back into the cubicle to retrieve her things, Sabrina turned to face Aubrey. Too excited to hold back, she grinned and raised two victorious fists. "Sold!"

"You're kidding!" Aubrey and Jenny both exclaimed.

Sabrina held a finger to her mouth for silence as Jocelyn burst from behind the fitting-room curtain and charged toward the cash register. Impressively maintaining a demeanor of perfect poise, Aubrey rang up the sale and bagged Jocelyn's old clothes. As the manager pulled out a pair of scissors to remove the price tags, the deliriously happy Jocelyn spun around and bolted down the aisle, promising to return soon. Jenny barely escaped being bowled over as the girl barreled by her.

Still grinning broadly, Sabrina rushed back to the counter. "So what time should I be here tomorrow?"

Whether stunned by the ludicrous sight of Jocelyn Harrington running out of the store with price tags flying or by Sabrina's unexpected flair for sales, Aubrey's vacant gaze remained fastened on the door.

"Ms. Holcomb?" Sabrina waved her hand in front of Aubrey's glazed eyes. "What time tomorrow?"

Aubrey slowly turned her head. "Time? Uh— ten will be fine. Just fine."

"I'll be here!" Grabbing her bag, Sabrina raced off before fate, foe, or the mysterious stuttering syndrome returned to foil her success.

"What was that all about?" Jenny asked when Sabrina skidded to a stop beside the fountain.

"It's a long story." Breathless with excitement and fatigue after her ordeal, Sabrina sank onto a stone bench. "I almost didn't get the job because my jeans don't fit right and I started stuttering and falling all over myself when Libby and her faithful sidekicks came in."

"Libby came in?" Sighing, Jenny sat beside her. "She can be such a jerk."

"Yeah, well. She's spending the weekend at Toy Town. I'll be hanging out at Too Chic Boutique because Jocelyn Harrington never buys anything, but she did today. From me. How'd your interview go?"

"No problem. I read books and that's all Mrs. Jenkins wanted to know." Jenny scowled. "That outfit looked totally awful on that girl, you know."

Sabrina nodded. "We know that, but she doesn't. As long as the customer's happy, nothing else matters, right?"

"I guess. At least, people who buy books don't know whether they're happy or not until *after* they've read them. Then they blame the author, not the person who sold it to them. And books can't be returned." Jenny shot Sabrina a worried sidelong glance. "But don't be surprised if that girl comes back demanding a refund."

Sabrina frowned. She wasn't worried about Jocelyn coming back. No matter what mirror she looked into when she was wearing her new outfit, her mind would perceive the image it had registered at the store, because that's what Jocelyn wanted to see. Minds were curious that way. No, what bothered her was that she had forgotten to take the spell off the mirror in the store.

But she wasn't about to tempt fate by going back into Too Chic now. Removing the spell would have to wait until the morning. She just hoped that if the store was busy tonight, Aubrey Holcomb had the stamina to handle the rush of satisfied shoppers. Everyone who looked into the enchanted glass would see themselves looking more alluringly attractive than they had ever dared dream.

Aubrey might even be *glad* to see her tomorrow.

Unless she started stammering like a blithering idiot again.

After confirming that Jenny would meet her and Harvey later at The Slicery, Sabrina took off for home. If she had contracted some weird kind of temporary witch's disease, her aunts would know what to do so she wouldn't suffer a relapse of the annoying and embarrassing symptoms. Besides, she couldn't wait to tell them about the

Teen Work Weekend project. They took great pride in everything they had achieved the hard way—like most people who weren't endowed with magical powers and had no choice. Zelda was a theoretical chemical physicist with degrees from M.I.T. and CalTech, who had once been in the running for a Nobel prize. Her not-nearly-as-serious, zany Aunt Hilda practiced the violin with a passion that matched any struggling mortal musician's dedication to perfecting his art. They'd be absolutely ecstatic to hear that their fledgling-witch niece was joining the labor force—even if only for two days.

Jogging up the front walk, Sabrina threw open the front door and jumped inside with a fervent squeal. "I got a job!"

Two things immediately grabbed her attention.

The stunning girl in flowing blue pants and matching jacket from the mall was standing in the foyer. Arching one delicately plucked eyebrow, she pointed at a spot in the air over Sabrina's head.

"Do tell."

Sabrina gasped with outraged surprise as a deluge of ice-cold water drenched her from above.

Chapter 4

Sputtering and speechless, Sabrina wiped water out of her eyes and looked up to see a hovering overturned bucket. Her response was instant and spontaneous, a defensive reflex she executed without thinking. Whipping out her finger, Sabrina *shoved* the strange girl.

Another startled gasp escaped her as *she* flew backward instead. The rebounding force of her own spell shot her out the open door to land on the hard wooden porch.

What in the Other Realm was happening here?

Angry and confused but very wary, Sabrina dragged herself to her feet and glared at the girl. The girl stared back, silently daring her to try something. Sabrina wisely refrained from escalating the conflict. The girl was obviously a witch and much more advanced in the practical applications of witchcraft than she was. Compounding that was the unsettling realization that she exercised her powers without compunction or regard for her innocent victims. Sabrina hadn't done anything to harm or upset her. They hadn't even spoken!

Remembering the girl's subtle points in Too Chic Boutique, gestures Sabrina had interpreted as requests for assistance, it seemed reasonable to assume that the maddeningly attractive, composed girl was responsible for the stammering staggers that had afflicted her there, too.

The disturbing question was—*why?*

"Sabrina?" Aunt Hilda called out as she started down the stairs. "Is that you?"

Perfect timing, Sabrina thought with a quick glance toward the stairs. She didn't know who the girl was or what she was doing in her house, but she was positive the young witch's powers were no match for Aunt Zelda's and Aunt Hilda's. A small puddle formed around Sabrina's feet as water dripped from her hair and clothes, evidence of the girl's callous treatment of their favorite niece. Although it was often irritating and inconvenient, her aunts were very strict about using magic with wisdom and without malice. They would not tolerate such irresponsible and cruel behavior.

Except they wouldn't have a clue the girl had used her powers to torment a total stranger!

With a casual flick of her finger, the girl removed the suspended bucket and puddles, then dried Sabrina's hair and clothes.

"What's this about a job?" Zelda asked as she came out of the kitchen into the living room. To Sabrina's dismay, she wasn't at all surprised to see the strange girl standing in the front hall. "Oh, you're back, too, Tanya. Did you enjoy the mall?"

Sabrina stepped back inside with a sinking sensation in her stomach. The evidence of the girl's treachery had been destroyed. It was her word against Tanya's and it would be really lame to accuse her aunts' guest of cruel and unwarranted harassment without proof.

"I see shopping the mortal way didn't *bore* you to death." Hilda's eyes narrowed as she glanced at Tanya and murmured under her breath, "A pity."

"On the contrary." Tanya spoke in a low voice that was all the more cutting because of its velvety tone. She directed her cold gaze at Sabrina and smiled. "It was quite educational."

Sabrina bristled, but managed to keep her own voice deceptively calm, too. "Who are you?"

"Oh, I'm sorry, Sabrina." Zelda gently gripped the girl's shoulders. "This is Tanya, a distant cousin. She's going to be staying with us for a while."

"Staying?" Sabrina felt the blood drain from her face. *No way! Not in my lifetime!* The objections she screamed in her head came out of her mouth in a shocked whisper, edited in tone and content. "Staying here? Really. For how long?"

"Too long," Hilda mumbled, then abruptly changed the subject. "I want to hear all about your job, Sabrina! In the kitchen. I can't stand"—Zelda shot her a warning look and Hilda took the hint—"crowds."

"Are you coming, Tanya?" Zelda asked as Hilda grabbed Sabrina's hand and yanked her around the living-room corner. "I just finished baking a chocolate cake with cream filling that is absolutely calorie-free."

"Baked? In one of those oven contraptions? How quaint, but no thanks. I'll order in from Paris if I get hungry." Covering a yawn, Tanya stretched, then moved toward the stairs. "If it's all right with you, I think I'll just go up to our room and rest awhile."

"Our room!" Sabrina hissed as Hilda pushed her through the kitchen door. Energized by anxious desperation, she immediately began pacing. "I'm not sharing my room with that—that—witch!"

"You don't have a choice." Drawing a huge knife from the butcher block, Hilda wrapped both hands around the hilt. She raised it over her head and brought it down with a resounding *whack,* severing Zelda's cake into two perfect halves. "Which piece do you want?"

"I'm not hungry." Scowling, Sabrina fell into a chair and folded her arms over her chest.

"Nonsense. There's no better excuse for over-indulging in chocolate than when you're faced with a terrible problem you can't do anything about." Sliding one half of the cake onto a plate, Hilda wiped away the excess filling squishing out between layers with her finger, then licked off the cream. "Delicious."

"I'm glad somebody appreciates it," Zelda said as she stormed in and sat down beside Sabrina. "Quaint, my eye."

"She finally got to you, too, huh?" Delighted, Hilda joined them at the table and took a vicious stab at the cake with her fork.

"Okay." Her aunts' obvious and mutual distress did not elude Sabrina. "What's the deal? Where did this Tanya person come from? More important, why is she *here?* And why can't we do anything about it?"

"You explain it, Zelda. I can't, not without choking on the words. Besides, my mouth is about to be full of cake and it's not polite to chew and shout at the same time."

"That's not fair, Hilda."

Sabrina shifted her gaze between them, wishing one of them would explain something.

"There's no such thing as fair in Tanya's family unless the reference applies to how one of their many hapless victims is doing." Hilda chewed, swallowed, and brutally hacked off another piece of the hapless cake. "As I recall, we didn't *fare* well at all when her father stayed with us in Rome that awful summer."

"What summer was that?" Sabrina asked, hoping to get the conversation moving forward.

"The summer of sixty-two, I think." Zelda frowned thoughtfully.

"Nineteen sixty-two? Eighteen sixty-two?" Shortly after moving in and finding out she was a witch like her aunts, Sabrina had learned to ask for clarification on things that didn't require explanation from mortals. Such as which century they were talking about.

"No, just sixty-two," Hilda said.

Or millennium, as the case may be. Sabrina sighed.

Squinting to jog her memory, Hilda waved her fork. "I remember because Nero married that arrogant little twit, Poppaea Sabina, after he had his first wife, Octavia, murdered."

"I'm still not convinced he did it," Zelda said.

"Of course he did!" Hilda scoffed. "He was a depraved jerk with absolute power and no moral values whatsoever."

"The Nero?" Sabrina sat back. "The one who burned down Rome?"

"Now, *that* he didn't do," Zelda said emphatically. "Quintus Jefferius did."

"Never heard of him."

"Tanya's father, Cousin Jeffrey. Or Lizard Wizard, if you prefer. We did." Hilda flinched when Zelda nudged her, but kept on talking. "After we learned to protect ourselves so he couldn't turn us into a matched team for his chariot anymore, he got bored."

"Tanya's father turned you into horses?" Appalled, Sabrina inhaled sharply. "And burned down Rome 'cause he was bored?"

Zelda shrugged. "Actually, I think he started the fire because he was mad. We were the favorites to win the Emperor's Handicap at the Coliseum."

"Two-to-one odds. We would have whipped the togas off the competition." Taking another, smaller bite, Hilda smiled. "Revenge is sweeter than chocolate. Jeffrey never forgave us."

"Then why are we stuck with Tanya?" Sabrina's voice cracked with stress.

"That's a good question." Hilda winced and Sabrina suspected Zelda had kicked her under the table.

"Her parents are worried because she spends too much time in the Other Realm," Zelda said gently. "She needs to be exposed to this world so she can see how difficult life is for mortals. Otherwise, she'll never learn to respect them. And the experience will be much more effective if she shares it with someone her own age."

"Like me?"

Both women nodded, but Hilda didn't meet her eye.

"I don't think so." Sabrina desperately tried to

beg off. "Respect is not a concept Tanya understands. Trust me, I know. Like father, like daughter."

"How could you possibly know that, Sabrina?" Zelda asked impatiently. "You just met the girl."

"Just a feeling?" Sabrina considered telling them about the bucket of water and Tanya's stuttering stumble spell, but somehow she didn't think it would make any difference.

"This is not a matter of choice," Zelda said sternly. "You can both benefit from getting to know each other. We promised Jeffrey, and you'll just have to make the best of it."

"I really think you should be more concerned about *what* Tanya will *make* of me."

"She's got a point," Hilda muttered.

"You're not making this any easier, Hilda," Zelda snapped.

Startled by Zelda's cross tone and Hilda's nod of submission, Sabrina realized that ing was futile and quickly reviewed her options. There weren't any. Except to do as they asked. Therefore, the sooner she gave Tanya a taste of mortal life, the sooner she'd be rid of her.

"Just one more question."

"Shoot." Hilda still avoided looking at her directly, which didn't help her nerves.

"What if I do everything I can to help Tanya understand and respect mortals, but she still doesn't get it? Are we stuck with her until she does?"

Zelda opened her mouth to respond, but Hilda beat her to the punch.

"Not necessarily." Hilda grinned.

Zelda sighed, but let her sister have the last word. "Now what's all this about a job?"

Sabrina's spirits brightened as she explained the Teen Work Weekend project. Her enthusiasm quotient rose by several degrees when she realized the job gave her a perfectly good excuse for *not* spending the entire weekend with Tanya.

"That's true," Zelda agreed, "but you won't be working all the time. What are you doing tonight?"

"I was going to meet Jenny and Harvey at The Slicery." Sabrina paused, stricken as a dozen horrendous and gruesome scenarios, the results of Tanya's malicious meddling, flashed through her mind: Jenny with green hair and buckteeth; pizzas topped with bats' wings and eye of newt; Harvey paying attention to Tanya because Tanya had made her invisible and mute. . . .

The most beautiful reptiles have the deadliest bites!

"But I can cancel!" Jumping up, Sabrina dashed for the phone. A deft wag of Zelda's finger snagged her shirt and pulled her back as she reached for the receiver.

"Or you could take Tanya with you," Zelda suggested. "It's a wonderful opportunity to introduce her to your friends and show her what you do for fun. You really *must* give her a chance."

Beaten, Sabrina nodded. Since there was no way out, the only logical thing to do was accept the situation and meet the challenge head-on. So she and Tanya had gotten off to a bad start. For all she knew, Tanya had good reasons for acting like—a witch. Maybe she had a boyfriend back in the Other Realm and was just angry because her parents made her leave. Her actions might even have been prompted by deep-seated feelings of insecurity. After all, Tanya was the new kid in an unfamiliar mortal neighborhood, which gave them something in common. Sabrina was not only the new kid in town, she had achieved the dubious distinction of being despised by the school's most popular and powerful girl. In fact, she thought as she headed toward the stairs, since both of them were teenaged girls *and* witches, they probably had a *lot* in common. There were a lot of witch-exclusive problems she couldn't discuss with anyone, not even Jenny. . . .

"Have you seen Salem?" Hilda's worried voice carried from the kitchen.

Suddenly frantic, Sabrina ran up the stairs and barged into her room.

Salem was lounging on the bed, purring in high gear as Tanya scratched him behind the ears. "A little more to the left. . . . Ahhh, yesssss."

Tanya didn't speak or bother to look up.

Shoving her hands in her front pockets, Sabrina rocked back on her heels. *So the cat didn't need to be rescued,* she thought sheepishly. And maybe Tanya was ignoring her because she was sorry about what happened earlier and didn't know what to say. Sabrina decided to give her the benefit of the doubt. "You two seem to be getting along."

Salem sighed, his black tail twitching with feline contentment. "Magic fingers are hard to resist, Sabrina. Especially when they're attached to such a beautiful witch. It almost makes giving up world conquest to become a cat worth it."

"That's not exactly honest, Salem. You didn't give up the world to become a cat. You were turned into a cat because you wanted to rule the world." Perching on the edge of the chair by the turret window, Sabrina tried to break the ice with Tanya. "You can't believe a word he says most of the time. And he's got this incredibly awful habit of making phone calls and pretending to be someone I really want to talk to—"

"Like Harvey." Salem chuckled.

"Right. Cats can be so annoying—"

"Must you babble?" Tanya graced Sabrina with a look of undisguised disgust.

"Am I? Babbling, I mean. Yeah, I guess I am." Sabrina sighed and shut up. It was going to be really hard to get to know each other if they didn't speak. Since friendly small talk obviously wasn't welcome, a more direct approach was necessary. "I don't mean to be rude, Tanya, but—what is your problem?"

"My problem?" Tanya laughed. "I don't have a problem, Sabrina. You do."

"Really? And what's that?"

"You're half mortal." Shaking out her long, luxurious hair, Tanya slid off the bed. Salem was dozing and didn't notice. "And I'm not."

"Meaning?" The hairs on the back of Sabrina's neck rose as Tanya's icy blue gaze bored into her.

"Meaning my magic is infinitely stronger than yours."

"Why is that a problem? Harvey's a faster runner than I am and Jenny reads Tolstoy for fun, but we're still friends."

"Why?" With a sudden flick of her finger, Tanya transformed the sleeping Salem into a stuffed cat made of shocking pink plush.

Sabrina leaped to her feet. "Turn him back—"

Tanya yawned as she pointed her wicked finger at Sabrina.

"—right now!" Sabrina's voice suddenly became a coarse rasp and her insides burned as an intense heat radiated outward from her chest through her arms and legs. She turned, looked in the mirror, and stifled a horrified cry as she watched herself wither into a stooped and shriveled, wrinkled, gray-haired, ancient hag.

"That's why," Tanya said.

Chapter 5

☆

Sabrina's first reaction was to scream in horrified indignation.

She didn't.

Losing her cool would be playing right into Tanya's hands.

Sinking gracefully into the turret-window chair, Tanya casually crossed her long, elegant legs and watched with an expression of mild curiosity.

Sabrina was not fooled by the girl's attitude of bored disdain. The despicable Tanya would like nothing better than to reduce her half-mortal cousin into a cowed, groveling wimp pathetically pleading for her lost youth. She wasn't going to get that satisfaction.

Bracing herself, Sabrina stared at the reflection

of herself as an old crone. Dark age spots dotted her withered face and the balding places visible under her thinning gray hair. A long, dark hair grew out of an ugly wart on her chin and her watery eyes were mere slits lost in the wrinkled folds of dry, cracked skin. She had shrunk a full two inches and the rose-colored T-shirt and snug jeans hung loosely on her bony frame.

Determined not to panic, Sabrina considered her limited options. Trying to change herself back would be a waste of time and energy. It wasn't a question of which witch was more powerful. Nobody but Tanya could reverse Tanya's spell. Assuming that she could, casting her own terrible spell on Tanya wouldn't work, either. Convinced she was superior, Tanya might accept a fate worse than death rather than admit Sabrina was her equal. Out of spite, she might decide to slither through life as a snake rather than remove the aging spell.

Which left Sabrina—and Salem—with nothing to rely on but her wits.

Mind over magic . . .

"So that's what I'll look like in ten thousand years," Sabrina croaked in her aged, sandpaper voice. She smiled, but didn't flinch when she saw that half her teeth were missing. The ones she had left were stained and broken. She also ignored the arthritic pain in her joints as she placed her clawed crone's hands on her protruding hipbones and cocked her head.

"Not exactly," Tanya purred, betraying a perverse sense of pleasure. "That's what you'll look like *for* the next ten thousand years."

New plan. Quickly! Sabrina knew there had to be a chink in Tanya's arrogant armor. Her mind raced, going back over everything that had occurred since their first encounter at Too Chic Boutique. Tanya could have left the store without removing the stuttering spell, but she hadn't. And, Sabrina realized with a sudden jolt of hope, she had been very quick to undo the water damage before Zelda and Hilda found her dripping on the porch!

"Okay, but—" Shrugging caused a shooting pain to arrow through Sabrina's shoulder. She rubbed the inflamed joint for dramatic effect and hobbled across the room. "I don't think my aunts will approve."

Silence.

Moaning, Sabrina placed her hand on her aching back and lowered herself onto the bed. Sighing, she picked up Salem's shocking pink, fiber-filled body and cradled him in her scrawny arms. "They're rather fond of Salem, too."

As though on cue, Hilda came thumping up the stairs. "Sabrina! Is Salem with you?"

Fixing Tanya with a toothless grin, Sabrina answered, "Yes! But you'll have to come in and get him!"

Eyes widening in alarm, Tanya flicked her finger toward Sabrina, then the cat.

Sabrina relaxed as a radiant heat spread through her aching muscles and bones, transforming her back into a teenager. The threat of her aunts' displeasure was all the ammunition she needed to survive Tanya the Terrible.

Salem re-formed with every hair on his back and tail fluffed out in feline terror. Hissing and spitting, he sprang off the bed and bolted out the door the instant Hilda opened it.

"What's wrong with him?" Hilda asked.

Tanya stared at the floor, silently seething.

"Must have been something he ate," Sabrina said. Salem could snitch if he wanted, but she wasn't going to add to Tanya's list of grievances. "He was stuffed."

"Tuna overdose, no doubt. So—" Leaning on the doorjamb, Hilda glanced at the girls. "How are you two getting along?"

"Just ragin'," Tanya muttered sarcastically.

"Ragin'?"

"It's a kid thing," Sabrina explained. "You know, like awesome, cool. Very—appropriate."

"Uh-huh. I'm sorry, Sabrina, but you'll have to point up your own dinner tonight. Zelda's presenting her paper at the university physics symposium and I promised I'd go."

"The one about quantum multiverse dynamics she's been working on the past few weeks?" Slipping off the bed, Sabrina knelt and pulled her magic book out from under it. She had some emergency research to do and she wanted the book safely in hand while Aunt Hilda was present to act as a deterrent. Her aunts were her only line of defense until she learned how to protect herself from Tanya.

"That's the one. Gotta go. Have fun at The Slicery. And don't stay out too late." Hilda eyed the book, but didn't comment as she moved back into the hall.

"The Slicery?" Tanya looked up with interest. "Is that one of those guts-and-gore horror movies?"

Sabrina blinked, aghast at the thought. When it came to insidious mayhem, Tanya was doing fine on her own. She didn't need any inspiration. "No, it's a pizza place. We'll play a little Foosball, hang out with my friends . . ."

"How thrilling. I'd rather sleep."

Sabrina couldn't resist the opening. "You don't *have* to go. I mean, computer pinball and pizza are so mundane—"

"But on second thought—" Tanya's calculating smile was not reassuring. "My parents sent me here to study mortals. I really can't pass up such an ideal opportunity."

"Of course not." Clutching her book, Sabrina nodded. "Do you want to eat before we go?"

"No. I don't eat home-pointed food. I'm going to take a nap. I don't want to be too tired to *thoroughly* enjoy my first mortal social outing." Brandishing her finger with a flourish, Tanya changed the bed and her clothes. Wearing a satin nightgown, she eased between the satin sheets and gossamer blanket that had replaced Sabrina's cotton sheets and blue bedspread. "Wake me when it's time to go."

"I'll be sure and sound the alarm." Resigned, Sabrina turned to leave.

"And, Sabrina," Tanya said softly. "Your aunts can't protect you from everything."

Rushing out of the room, Sabrina ran down the stairs. Maybe she could talk Aunt Hilda and Aunt Zelda into stopping by The Slicery on their way home from the symposium. At the moment, they were the only ones standing between her and total devastation by Tanya. It couldn't hurt to ask. Being bored always made Aunt Hilda hungry, and scientific speeches always bored her. In fact, Sabrina couldn't imagine why her fun-loving aunt had agreed to go to Aunt Zelda's presentation at all. Her usual response to such invitations was, "I'd rather die." And she meant it.

"Hello?" Sabrina dashed through the empty living room into the kitchen. "Aunt Hilda? Aunt Zelda?"

"They're out of here." Whiskers twitching, Salem poked his head out of the dry-goods cabinet. "Is the coast clear?"

"She's asleep." Dropping the magic book on the table, Sabrina went to the counter and cut herself a large piece of cake. "I can't believe they left without saying good-bye! They've never done that before."

"There's a first time for everything." Stepping onto the floor, Salem paused to give his ruffled fur a few quick licks.

"And whatever made Aunt Hilda decide to go to a physics symposium anyway?" Falling into a chair, Sabrina attacked the cake with aggravated gusto.

"There's a first time for everything."

Sabrina shot Salem a questioning look as he leaped onto the chair beside her. "Are you a double?"

"No. I lost my ability to duplicate myself when I became a cat."

"Then why are you repeating yourself?" Sabrina asked, still suspicious. Doubles could be programmed to say only three things.

"Was I? No reason." Salem distracted himself with a concentrated study of his claws, extending and retracting them several times to test the needle-sharp points. "Maybe I can get in one good swipe before the wicked witch turns me into a marshmallow bunny."

"Wouldn't it be safer to just make yourself scarce until Tanya leaves? Or make sure you're always in the same room with Aunt Hilda or—" Seized by a sudden flash of brilliance, Sabrina laughed. "That's it! That's why, isn't it, Salem?"

"Hmm? What's what?"

"Don't play dumb cat with me! Aunt Hilda went with Aunt Zelda so they wouldn't be around to protect me from Tanya! Right?"

Salem blinked. "There's a first time for everything."

"Right!" Sabrina's elation at solving the riddle of Aunt Hilda's sudden interest in science fizzled abruptly. *I'm on my own with Tanya!* "What am I going to do?"

"Fix a tuna casserole for dinner, I hope. Can I lick the can?"

"About Tanya! You know what happened up there, Salem?" Sabrina glanced at the ceiling. "She turned you into pink plush and me into an old hag for no reason except to prove that she could!"

"Yeah. So?"

"So? She'll probably turn me into a warthog at The Slicery just to impress my friends. It took six weeks before the manager would let me back in after *you* stowed away in my bag! I don't think he'll overlook a wild, stinky pig!"

"There's no need to get hysterical."

"Yes. There is. I'm new at this witch stuff *and* half mortal. I'm no match for her!"

"Who told you that?" Salem asked, but there was an edge of caution in his deep voice. "Besides Tanya."

Sabrina hesitated. "No one. Why?"

"Oh, just curious." Salem hummed softly as his green gaze absently scanned the room.

"Are you saying I've got just as much power as she does?"

"I'm not saying anything." Salem looked furtively toward the stairs that led up to the linen closet, gateway to the Other Realm and the Witch's Council. "Not a word."

Sabrina wasn't dense. There was more to Tanya's sudden, unannounced visit than anyone was allowed to say. She just had to figure out what. "Okay. If I assume our powers are equal, can I also assume there's a way to get back at her?"

Salem just stared at her.

"Not even if she decides to do something really awful to one of my mortal friends?"

"No witch can undo another witch's sealed spell without special dispensation from the Witch's Council, Sabrina."

"Oh, yeah." Recent experience had certainly driven that particular point home. Sabrina frowned, pondering the problem. "So my only recourse is offense rather than defense."

Jumping onto the table, Salem sat down, glanced upward again, and sighed. "Life is a *learning* experience. *How* you handle it is—your business, Sabrina."

"It's a test!" Sabrina started as Salem squeezed his eyes closed and cringed, as though he were expecting to be struck down by some unseen powerful hand. When nothing happened after a few seconds, he flopped down on his side, closed his eyes, and sighed again—with relief.

Troubled, Sabrina resisted the urge to ask the cat any more questions. Although he hadn't said much, it didn't take a genius to figure out that the vague hints he had given her had been spoken at great risk to himself. She just wasn't sure what they meant, only that she was probably being tested for something, and caution was advised.

A test for what? Taking another bite of cake, Sabrina chewed slowly and swallowed hard. *How am I supposed to study?* The next bite never hit her mouth. As she raised her fork, her gaze settled on the book. The fork clattered on her plate as she dropped it and yanked the huge leather-bound volume toward her.

Witch against witch. There's gotta be a reference. Nibbling her lip, she searched the index until she found the page numbers. However, when she flipped the book open, the pages were blank. "What kind of a dorky textbook is this?"

"Not a word . . ." Salem mumbled in his sleep.

"Not even from the book? That's not fair!" Dust billowed from the ancient pages as Sabrina slammed the book closed. Coughing, she stomped over to the prim and proper portrait of Aunt Louisa, and froze. The elderly woman's stern, thin-lipped mouth was covered with a painted zipper.

Sabrina groaned, indulging herself in a moment of anguished despair. She was, apparently, engaged in some kind of test, a rite of passage that was so secret, even its purpose was a complete mystery. She didn't have a clue what to expect or what was expected of her. Her aunts were deliberately absent. The cat was asleep. The pertinent text was missing from the book, and the portrait wasn't talking.

And she was about to unleash Tanya on her unsuspecting, defenseless friends.

Chapter 6

Walk! You expect me to walk?" Tanya balked at the front door. "You can't be serious!"

Sighing with frustration, Sabrina reminded herself that Tanya was experiencing major culture shock. Patience was imperative. They were already fifteen minutes late because Tanya had not been able to refuse the challenge Sabrina had cleverly devised as a means of self-defense: that she *wouldn't* be able to master doing things the mortal way. The ploy had worked to a degree. Spoiled and totally dependent on magic for everything, Tanya had been too distracted by the difficulties of dressing herself to cast any more annoying spells.

Plastering a sympathetic smile on her face, Sabrina turned to face her stricken cousin. She had ditched the rose pullover in favor of a beige blouse with long, billowing sleeves, but she was still wearing jeans. Given her choice of everything in Sabrina's closet, Tanya had selected her favorite outfit: black tights, laced ankle boots, and a long, shimmering gold tunic top, all of which she had finally managed to pull on, zip, button, and lace up. Pressed for time and pushing her luck, Sabrina had relented and let the girl apply makeup and do her hair with magic. The results were depressingly dazzling. Although Tanya's poise had slipped with the realization that doing things the mortal way was not a snap, she was strikingly beautiful.

Maybe Harvey won't notice . . .

"It's only a few blocks. Mortals without cars *have* to walk if they want to get anywhere. Some people even take walks for fun."

"But it's so primitive!"

"True," Sabrina agreed. "But just think how proud your parents will be when they find out you actually got from one place to another using your own two feet!"

Discretion being another safe defense, Sabrina had not informed Tanya that she hadn't yet quite mastered instantaneous transportation from one location to another. Her aunts had assured her it was just a question of time and practice. Until then, her destination accuracy wasn't refined beyond a limited range. Zapping herself into the heart of Africa or to the top of Mount Everest might have been too tempting. Realistically, assuming she didn't pop herself over the side of a cliff or into a pride of hungry lions, she'd still be hard-pressed to get back anytime soon. Certainly not in time to go to work in the morning.

"An excellent point." Inhaling deeply to steel herself for the trial ahead, Tanya moved sedately across the porch and down the steps.

As she hurried to catch up, Sabrina had to give the girl credit. At least for the moment, Tanya was as determined to overcome the obstacles of mortal existence as Sabrina was to survive her association with Tanya relatively unscathed. So far, she was holding her own, but only because Tanya's sense of superiority made it possible to manipulate her. The do-it-like-mortals maneuver was a perfect example, but she couldn't count on that to last for long. Sooner or later, Tanya would give up from frustration or boredom. And despite Salem's unspoken assurances to the contrary, Sabrina was pretty sure she'd come out the loser in a contest of dueling magic.

"This is actually rather invigorating." Incredibly pleased with herself, Tanya lengthened her stride.

"I've always thought so." Sabrina hustled to match the increased pace. When she caught up, Tanya suddenly surged forward again. Refusing to be baited into a race, Sabrina deliberately lagged behind. She hadn't told Tanya they might have been thrown together as part of some mysterious test, either. Knowing something Tanya didn't might also give her an advantage in a pinch. However, even though she didn't have a clue what the unconfirmed test was about, she seriously doubted if anyone cared who could walk faster.

Except Tanya.

"Wrong way!" Sabrina shouted as Tanya sped across the next intersection. Turning right, she kept on at her more leisurely pace until the girl drew abreast of her. "You can slow down now. We're here."

"This is it?" A look of distaste flashed across Tanya's face as she studied the rustic exterior of The Slicery. She quickly regrouped, forcing a smile as Sabrina opened the door. "You go first."

Sabrina hesitated.

"I don't know anyone, Sabrina. This is your territory, not mine."

"Right." Stepping inside with Tanya following close behind, Sabrina spotted Jenny waving from a corner table. Harvey was sitting with his back to the door. He turned, grinned, and almost dropped the piece of pizza he was holding. The buzz of conversation ceased suddenly and even the clanging pinball machines fell silent as everyone else in the room turned to stare, too.

Uh-oh! Sabrina winced, wondering if Tanya had given her blue skin or fangs or bug eyes when she wasn't looking. Then she realized that the local crowd wasn't staring at her. All eyes were on the statuesque, blue-eyed beauty standing beside her.

The admiring attention was not lost on Tanya, either. "You were right, Sabrina. I think I'm going to enjoy this."

Breathing easier, Sabrina led the way across the room. She skirted around the center tables keeping close to the wall, not because of Tanya, but to avoid passing too close to Libby and Cee Cee, who were sitting with three players from the Westbridge football team. In all fairness, she had to admit that Tanya was making an effort to stay within mortal parameters. However, her relief was a bit premature.

"Hey, gorgeous!" Larry Carson, hot hunk and star Westbridge quarterback, stood up and patted his vacated stool. "Why don't you have a seat over here? *You* are definitely in-crowd material."

Libby glowered at him, probably for daring to invite anyone to join them without her permission.

"No, thanks," Tanya said sweetly. "You have it." With a flip of her finger, she picked the husky blond boy off his feet and deposited him back on the high stool. Fortunately, no one but Larry seemed to realize he hadn't vaulted back into the seat himself.

"Maybe you should go out for gymnastics, too, Larry," one of his companions suggested.

Dazed and dumbfounded, Larry just nodded.

Libby stared at Tanya with an expression of curious respect. Any girl who had the confidence to brush off the attentions of Larry Carson was too cool to ignore.

Tapping Tanya on the arm, Sabrina hissed in her ear. "Mortal girls can't toss football players around like rag dolls!"

"But he was so crass!" Tanya hissed back.

Sabrina smiled. "I didn't say he didn't deserve it. I just meant that you can't be too obvious about using—you know? You get to go back to the Other Realm. I've gotta live here."

"Oh, right." Tanya nodded solemnly. "I'll try to remember."

Keeping her fingers crossed, Sabrina urged Tanya forward and slipped into the stool beside Harvey. "Sorry I'm late. Tanya, uh—dropped in unexpectedly. She's my cousin. I didn't think you'd mind if she joined us."

"Nope." Harvey smiled his charming smile and offered Tanya a slice of his pizza. "Double pepperoni."

"Oh, uh—thanks." Tanya hesitated, wrinkling her nose. "Is this pizza? It looks—interesting."

Jenny handed her a napkin. "Haven't you ever had pizza before?"

"She's led a sheltered life," Sabrina explained as Tanya eased a slice onto the napkin and took a tentative whiff. "In South America. A remote jungle village. Pizza's not real big down there."

"It's great, Tanya. You'll like it." Jenny laughed. "Believe me. Anyone who can make Larry Carson back off like he was hit by an eighteen-wheeler can handle pizza."

"Eighteen-wheeler?" Tanya bit off the pointy end and smiled as she chewed.

"It's a big truck," Harvey said. "Guess you didn't see many of those in the jungle, either."

"A truck!" An ominous scowl darkened Tanya's face as she whirled on Jenny and snapped her finger skyward. "You called me a truck?"

Sabrina winced as thunder boomed and lightning flashed outside. Digging in pockets for their car keys, four boys rushed out the door to roll up open car windows.

Unaware of how close she was to becoming whatever disgusting creature struck Tanya's infuriated fancy, Jenny smiled and hastened to explain. "No, not at all. That's just a figure of speech."

"A compliment," Sabrina added. "Because not everyone has the power to knock a quarterback off his feet."

"And it's about time someone did." Jenny rolled her green eyes. "Granted, he's a major hunk, but that's not a license to be totally crude. Which he is."

Calming down, Tanya eyed Jenny thoughtfully. "I could turn him into a monkey."

"Now *that* I'd like to see," Harvey quipped.

Sabrina jumped up and grabbed Tanya's hand

before she could point the dreaded finger of fate. "Foosball anyone?"

After ten minutes, Tanya lost all patience with trying to slide and twist wooden rods to bash a ball. Knowing Tanya's self-esteem could sustain only so much damage before her potentially cataclysmic temper took over, Sabrina didn't object when Tanya left to investigate the mechanical pinball machines. The girl's first foray into the mortal world playing by mortal rules was going better than Sabrina had dared hope. In the event that was all Cousin Jeffrey and the unconfirmed test required, she didn't want to interfere with the successful completion of Tanya's crash course. If Tanya ever hoped to pass as a mortal, she had to solo sometime. Accepting Harvey's challenge to another round of Foosball, Sabrina just kept a wary eye on her.

I hate Sabrina! Tanya released the trigger knob and tensed as the hammer struck the last of her small metal balls, shooting it onto the board.

And I hate pretending to be mortal! Pressing the buttons that controlled the gates, she gritted her teeth and grunted as she repeatedly whacked the ball away from the drop tray.

And I especially hate being nice! Every scoring bell and buzzer seemed to intensify her rage rather than appease it. She was a witch! She didn't *have* to do things the hard way! She didn't care what her parents thought! But Sabrina had tricked her, and once she had accepted the dare, pride left her with no choice but to follow through.

"Didn't I see you at the mall today?"

The intrusive voice ruined Tanya's concentration and the metal ball rolled unhindered through the gates. Losing the ball and the game ignited the fury that had been smoldering since she had fallen into Sabrina's calculated trap. But enough was enough. First she'd silence the rude girl behind her. Then she'd make Sabrina sorry. Raising her hand, Tanya turned.

Libby.

Tanya remembered the girl from the store and realized they shared a mutual passion. Like her, Libby despised Sabrina.

Amused by the idea of having a mortal ally, Tanya holstered her finger and smiled. "Yes, I think so. At the Too Chic Boutique, wasn't it?"

"That's right. You didn't stay long, either," Libby observed cautiously.

Tanya sighed. "No, it was such a ghastly experience. Cousin Sabrina's bumbling was just *so* embarrassing."

"She's your cousin?" Libby's hand flew to her chest as she gasped in disbelief. "No way. You're so sophisticated. Much too cosmopolitan to be related to someone who's so—"

"Pedestrian?"

"Exactly." Libby grinned, then feigned a concerned frown. "Not that she can help it, of course."

"No," Tanya agreed. "Still, she has no business working someplace where discerning, style-conscious people like yourself want to shop."

"That is so true." Libby's gaze flicked over Tanya's slim frame. "I mean, your outfit is absolutely right on. Sabrina's sense of fashion is severely retarded."

"Is it?" Tanya found this perception fascinating. Either Libby hadn't noticed or didn't care that Tanya was wearing Sabrina's clothes.

Nodding, Libby edged closer and whispered, "The job at Too Chic Boutique was supposed to be mine."

"Really? What a shame you didn't get it. You're obviously so much better suited for it than Sabrina."

Glancing around to make sure no one else was listening, Libby shielded her mouth with her hand. "I don't know how, but I suspect Sabrina rigged the draw. *She* got Too Chic and *I* got stuck with the toy store."

Faking appalled shock, Tanya inhaled sharply. "But that's cheating! And it's definitely not fair to you. . . ."

"Libby. I'm a cheerleader."

"Tanya. I should have guessed." Having baited the hook, Tanya prepared to reel in the catch. Sabrina's aunts would tell her parents if they thought she was responsible for anything awful that happened to Sabrina. And she wasn't about to risk being stripped of her magic and exiled to the mortal realm for a few decades as punishment. Libby had unwittingly provided her with the perfect means of revenge. However, in the event something went wrong, she had to make sure no one suspected her. It would be easy to place the blame on Libby, her mortal patsy.

A thin boy wearing glasses stepped up to the pinball machine beside them and started to drop his quarters.

"Get lost, creep!" Libby snapped.

The boy fled.

Impressed, Tanya motioned Libby closer. "Considering what happened at Too Chic today, it's entirely possible that Sabrina won't have that job too long."

"I should be so lucky."

"Can you meet me for lunch?"

Libby regarded Tanya evenly. "I don't start work until one. I'll meet you on the Food Court at noon."

"I'll be there." Tanya grinned. "And Libby—wear something smashing. Just in case there's a job opening at Too Chic Boutique. Tomorrow just might be your lucky day."

☆

Chapter 7

☆

Sabrina shifted uncomfortably when Tanya returned to the table. Libby had instigated their conversation and they hadn't talked long, but Tanya had smiled a lot. That alone made the situation suspicious.

"So did you have better luck with pinball?" Jenny asked brightly.

"Actually, yes." Tanya scowled. "I was doing just fine until that incredibly rude girl interrupted and made me lose my last ball."

And you didn't blast her into another dimension? Surprised, Sabrina sat back slightly. Tanya was making remarkable progress. Still, learning to control her temper didn't necessarily mean Tanya had conquered the self-indulgent arrogance that triggered the tantrums. On the other hand, if Libby couldn't provoke her into losing her resolve, there was hope.

"What time do you have to be at work tomorrow, Sabrina?" Harvey asked.

"Ten." Sabrina beamed, unable to control the warm flush she always felt when Harvey shyly looked into her eyes. "How about you?"

"Ten for me, too." Nodding, Harvey paused a moment. "What time do you get done?"

"Not until five."

Tanya's intensely curious, blue-eyed gaze shifted back and forth between them.

Amused, Jenny shook her head.

Sabrina knew the exchange sounded inane, but she and Harvey were still in the awkward stages of their blossoming relationship. Neither one wanted to appear as if he was taking the other's interest for granted. "What time do you finish?"

"Three. I thought we could catch a movie, but if you're not going to be done—"

"I'd love to see a movie, but I hate going by myself." Tanya sighed, then glanced at Harvey. "I'll be all alone while Sabrina's working, too. Maybe you and I could go—"

Harvey looked up. "Well, we could—"

Tanya waved her finger at Sabrina.

No, you can't! The words reverberated through Sabrina's head, but nothing came out of her mouth.

"—as long as Sabrina doesn't mind," Harvey finished.

I mind! Caught completely off guard, Sabrina couldn't believe Tanya had actually implemented one of her imagined scenarios. Could Tanya read minds, or what? She was mute! But at least, she wasn't invisible—yet.

"Sabrina doesn't mind, do you?" Tanya didn't even bother to look at her. "See?"

Jenny frowned uncertainly as Sabrina shook her head. Then, since Harvey might interpret that as consent, she nodded. That didn't work, either.

"Okay. Cool. Do you like action-adventure, Tanya? *The Malibu Marauder* starts at three-fifteen." Harvey was so honest and naive, he didn't have a clue that something really weird was happening.

Jenny, however, seemed to sense that Tanya wanted a shot at her boyfriend.

She's probably wondering why I don't say something. Maybe she thinks I'm not worried. Besides, it would be really lame to object to my cousin going to a movie when I have to work.

Noticing Sabrina's frantic expression, Jenny took the hint. "I've been wanting to see that one, too!"

Tanya aimed her fearless finger at Jenny and fired.

"Why—hic—don't I—hic—meet you—hic, hic—" Throwing her hand over her mouth, Jenny jumped up and ran for the restroom.

That's it! Hiccups weren't nearly as humiliating as buckteeth and green hair, but Tanya had no right to toy with her friends. Period. Pushed to the limit, Sabrina retaliated. *Power perm and protein swirls, create a crown of frizzy curls!* She pointed with a vengeance.

Whooooshhh!

Sabrina felt a warm rush of air swirl around her head.

Harvey did a double take. "What happened to your hair, Sabrina?"

Tanya's dark hair still fell in shining, soft waves over her shoulders. With a smug smile, she waved her magic finger and removed the spell that had stolen Sabrina's voice. "Yes, Sabrina. What *did* happen to your hair?"

Stunned, Sabrina reached up and touched the dry frizzies flying away from her scalp in glorious disarray. Her carefully crafted spell had bounced back—again. How? That, she realized with a start, was hardly important at the moment. For one reckless second, she almost wished Tanya *had* made her invisible, too. Every eye in The Slicery was riveted on her frightfully bad hair.

Jumping off the stool, Sabrina glared at Tanya. "Jenny. Now."

Shrugging, Tanya waved toward the restroom.

A moment later, Jenny came out and hurried back to the table. "That was so bizarre! My hiccups stopped just like that—" Her eyes widened in bewildered shock. "Sabrina! What happened to your hair?"

"Humidity." Assured that Jenny's hiccups were cured, Sabrina glared at her shamelessly unconcerned cousin. Thoughtlessly acting on whatever whim served her selfish purposes, the girl was incorrigible and totally contemptuous of mortals. No one was safe.

"Let's go, Tanya. We're out of here." Sabrina turned and stormed toward the door.

"Where are you going?" Jenny called after her.

"Home! To soak my head!"

Sabrina sat on the edge of the bathtub, nursing her wounded pride and her magic-damaged hair. This was the third application of superprotein conditioner she had tried since locking herself in the bathroom over an hour ago, after Tanya had gone to sleep in her bed. This time the treatment had to work. She was out of conditioner and she didn't dare try a counterspell until she figured out what was going on. The risk of accidentally turning her frizzed hair into color-coded wire or plastic brush bristles was just too great. Frizzies could be explained, although she doubted Aubrey Holcomb would be terribly pleased. But flyaway hair or not, she was going to work at Too Chic Boutique in the morning.

For a lot of reasons.

She wouldn't have to cope with Tanya for several hours.

The job was too good an opportunity to pass up.

And she didn't want Libby to get it by default.

Rising stiffly, Sabrina stepped up to the mirror over the sink. Squishing her fingers through the green cream coating her head, she decided to rinse. A few more minutes wouldn't make much difference and she was exhausted. Surely the stylish manager of Too Chic Boutique would prefer a perky employee with a bad perm over a sleep-deprived zombie with perfect tresses.

Maybe.

Libby was perky with perfect hair.

And she didn't have a witch of a cousin who was determined to ruin her life.

She just had a witch of a classmate who gave her an occasional rotten moment.

Turning on the shower, Sabrina felt a rare pang of remorse for some of the pranks she had pulled on the conceited cheerleader over the past several months. But disappearing man-dough dates, being temporarily turned into a pineapple, and hearing the absolute, although somewhat unflattering truth from her friends did not constitute a campaign of wanton destruction. Besides, Libby always *did* something that warranted reprisal.

Tanya had launched her reign of terror for no reason.

"Except that I was born half mortal. Prejudice definitely stinks."

Stepping into the tub, Sabrina washed the green gunk out of her hair. Unfortunately, the warm water couldn't wash away her troubled thoughts. Even so, she felt refreshed when she finished. And famished.

Slipping back into her robe and wrapping a towel around her wet hair, Sabrina quietly padded down to the kitchen. If a whole bottle of conditioner hadn't cured her frizzies, she didn't want to know about it just yet. She didn't want anything to disrupt her rendezvous with a few Tanya-free minutes of peace and quiet and another slice of Aunt Zelda's chocolate cake.

Except Aunt Hilda.

"You've got the midnight munchies, too, I see." Wearing her favorite nightgown, a tattered flannel that dated back to the turn of the century, Hilda sat at the table with a quart of ice cream and the rest of the cake. With a swish of her hand, she yanked open the silverware drawer and sent all the forks flying around the room. "Grab a fork!"

"Guess Aunt Zelda's lecture wasn't much fun, huh?" Snatching a fork as it sped by, Sabrina pulled up a chair and dug in.

"Want a spoon, too?"

Sabrina ducked as three forks zoomed over her head. "No, thanks. I'd rather live to see the sun rise."

"Oh, sorry." Pointing the renegade silverware back into the drawer, Aunt Hilda sighed. "Thunder and lightning didn't seem like such a good idea at this hour."

"I appreciate that. The longer Tanya sleeps, the better my chances are of going through life as a girl."

"That bad?" When Sabrina nodded, Hilda stopped eating to wince in grim sympathy. "How bad is that?"

Sabrina paused thoughtfully, then cocked her head to meet her aunt's worried gaze. "How bad was sitting through a presentation on quantum multiverse dynamics?"

Hilda's expression instantly changed from grim to pained. "About as bad as force-feeding artichokes to aardvarks because Drell thinks it's funny when they burp."

"That pretty much sums it up." Sabrina smiled despite her distressing circumstances. She didn't think Aunt Hilda had ever force-fed an aardvark, especially not to amuse her obnoxious ex-fiancé Drell, but the image had the desired effect. Her often-irreverent, sometimes too-frivolous, but always-concerned Aunt Hilda had a knack for cheering her up.

Sabrina also suspected Hilda wanted to help. "I don't suppose it would do any good to explain that Tanya almost turned the school's star quarterback into a monkey. Or that she's dedicated herself to making my life miserable."

"I wish there was something I could do to make this easier, but—" Hilda dug into the ice cream with her fork.

"I know. You can't. I got the message."

"There's some things you just have to figure out for yourself."

"It's all right, Aunt Hilda." Sabrina sighed. "I understand. I don't want you to get into trouble for breaking some weird witch's taboo. Rules are rules—"

"Exactly!" Nodding vigorously, Hilda dropped her fork and leaned forward for emphasis. "Some of them are written in stone and some—aren't."

Confused, Sabrina frowned. "What does that mean?"

Hilda shrugged. "Just because most witches follow an accepted—but not legally binding or enforced—code of conduct doesn't mean everyone does."

"Uh-huh. Could you be more specific?" Sabrina asked hopefully.

"Well—" Hilda paused, choosing her words carefully. "Most young witches go through a phase of harassing mortals because it's fun and they can."

Guilty as charged! Sabrina averted her gaze to dip into the ice cream. It was still frozen solid, compliments of Hilda's magic.

"But it gets old because it's boring," Hilda continued. "Where's the thrill when a witch has such a distinct advantage?"

That depends on the mortal, Sabrina thought. She couldn't honestly say she didn't feel a slight thrill whenever her magic got the best of Libby. Although getting the best of Libby on mortal terms *was* more gratifying.

"But another witch! Now *that's* a challenge." Eyes sparkling, Hilda watched Sabrina expectantly.

"It's a drag!"

"Not for Tanya."

"Well, that's certainly true, but hardly comforting." Rolling her eyes, Sabrina slumped despondently. "I'm just lucky people don't drive around in chariots anymore or I'd be stuffing myself with hay instead of cake and ice cream. In fact, the only thing that's probably saved me is that Tanya may not know her father turned you into a horse!" Sabrina rammed her fork into the cake.

"Sabrina," Hilda said pointedly. "I haven't been turned into a horse in two thousand years."

The cake-filled fork stopped in front of Sabrina's open mouth. "How—"

"Is the operative word. Be careful."

A flash of lightning followed by a thunderous boom shook the house.

"Time for bed!" With an apologetic glance upward, Hilda jumped up, magically cleared the table, and left.

Feeling more confused than she had since the first day she had found out she was a witch, Sabrina trudged up the stairs. She was too tired to think about the clues hidden in Aunt Hilda's and Salem's guarded comments. A good night's sleep was sure to put a different spin on things and clear her mind, even though she had to share the couch with Salem because Tanya had taken her bed.

Deciding to change into a nightgown before combing out her hair, Sabrina crept quietly into her room and across the floor. The door hinge squeaked softly as she opened the closet.

"Why don't you just turn on all the lights—"

Sabrina froze at the sound of Tanya's angry voice.

"—and blast me out of bed with the stereo!"

Without a hint of warning, Sabrina was thrown into the closet. The door slammed closed and the outside handle sizzled as Tanya fused it to lock her in. Exhausted and trapped, Sabrina sank to the floor, wrapped her arms around her knees, and sighed in dismal surrender.

Chapter 8

☆

"Now you've done it!" Salem hissed.

Sabrina flinched, startled by the unexpected voice from the back corner of the closet. "I thought you were going to sleep on the couch," she snapped in a harsh whisper, angry because Tanya had blindsided her again, and annoyed because Salem was a witness to this latest humiliation.

"That was my plan." The cat sighed. "Unfortunately, Tanya came in while I was getting my catnip mouse and foiled it. I decided starving in the closet was preferable to spending the next hundred years as a cast-iron doorstop."

"A wise decision, I'm sure." Tucking her legs underneath her, Sabrina curled into a ball and rested her head on her arm.

"What are you doing?"

"Going to sleep."

"You can't sleep now! You've got to get me out of here!" Salem mewed plaintively. "I'm hungry."

"We all have our problems, Salem, and right now I think mine are worse than yours." Sabrina shifted, trying to find a more comfortable position in the cramped closet. "I mean, it was bad enough just having Libby trying to make my life a nightmare. Now I've got Tanya lurking around every corner making *sure* it is!"

"Talk about crying over spilled milk," Salem grumbled, then moaned. "Milk!" Very heavy sigh. "Don't mind me, Sabrina. I'm just going to curl up in the corner and listen to my stomach growl. . . ."

Sabrina took a deep breath. Taking her frustrations out on the cat wasn't fair, and feeling sorry for herself wasn't accomplishing anything. Salem and Aunt Hilda had both risked the wrath of the Witch's Council to give her some helpful hints. The least she could do was *try* to figure out what they meant.

There's some things you just have to figure out for yourself. . . .

Aunt Hilda's words echoed in her mind as Sabrina sat up and dropped her chin in her hands. They were positive words in a strange, convoluted way because they indicated that she *could* figure things out.

I haven't been turned into a horse in two thousand years. . . .

Another bright light on the gloomy horizon. Aunt Hilda and Aunt Zelda had figured out how to protect themselves from Cousin Jeffrey. So there had to be a way for her to protect herself from Tanya. Taking heart, Sabrina reviewed everything that had happened since her ruthless cousin's arrival.

She couldn't be positive, but it was entirely probable that Tanya was responsible for the stumbling stutters she had been stricken with at Too Chic Boutique. There was *no* question that Tanya had drenched her with water and turned her into an ancient old crone. Or sabotaged her ability to talk, to wangle a movie invitation from Harvey. Not that Tanya was attracted to or interested in Harvey. Tanya's actions had been prompted solely because *Sabrina* was attracted to and interested in him.

But maybe things weren't nearly as futile as they appeared. Bolstered by a faint glimmer of hope, Sabrina continued her mental review.

Although Salem hadn't actually said so, the cat had strongly suggested that her magic was just as powerful as Tanya's. Being half mortal or a full-blooded witch wasn't a factor except in Tanya's mind. However, when she had tried to strike back, her spells bounced back on her, leaving Tanya unaffected.

"Like they rebounded *off* something," Sabrina muttered.

"What?" Salem asked sleepily.

"The spells I tried to use on Tanya. When I shoved her, I flew backward instead. And the bad-hair spell I threw at her gave *me* the frightful frizzies."

"Return to sender," Salem said distinctly.

"Yeah. It's like she's got this protective coating that repels spells—" Sabrina choked back a cry of joy. She didn't want to wake Tanya now that she might be on the verge of discovering a defense. "A shield! There's a shield spell or something, isn't there, Salem?"

"What do I know?" Salem said evasively. "I'm a cat."

"Right." Sabrina was sure she was on the right track, but she had to check the book, which was still in the kitchen where she had left it earlier.

"A very hungry cat."

"Stop pestering me, Salem. I can't get us out of here if you won't let me think."

Silence.

Conjuring a flashlight, Sabrina checked the cracks around the door. She couldn't counter Tanya's fusion spell on the handle, but she *could* remove the bolt between the door and the doorjamb. After pointing some oil into the squeaky hinges, she zapped out the bolt and eased the door open.

Salem dashed by her, across the room, and into the hall.

Tanya stirred slightly, but she didn't wake up.

Vulnerable until she learned how to create a shield, Sabrina eased the closet door closed behind her, then tiptoed to the bedroom door. Less than a minute later, she was back in the kitchen. After giving Salem some milk and tuna so she could concentrate in peace, she settled down at the kitchen table with the book.

Shields were listed in the index as a subtopic under witch against witch.

And all those pages had been blank when she had looked at them earlier.

Holding her breath, Sabrina quickly flipped the book open. The page was still blank.

"Not fair! Foul!"

"Now what?" Salem looked up from his bowl, whiskers twitching in exasperation.

"The shield spell isn't here! What good is a reference book that refuses to tell you what you want to know!"

"That book just has a warped sense of humor." Salem paused thoughtfully. "Try this. 'Shields up.'"

"Like on *Star Trek?* That is really dumb, Salem. We're talking magic here, not science fiction."

"Well, it works for them!" The cat huffed indignantly. "But if you've got a better idea . . ."

"All right!" Rolling her eyes, Sabrina looked at the book and mumbled, "Shields up."

"No, no, *no!* You gotta say it with feeling!" Salem leaped onto the table. "A Klingon Bird-of-Prey is about to attack and Tanya's in command. She just armed their photon torpedoes! Your phasers are off-line! Your ship's gonna be blown to smithereens—"

"Shields up!" Sabrina barked the order, then watched in fascination as the instructions for creating a shield against another witch's spell instantly appeared in bold black script. "Hey! It worked!"

"Brought to you by the wonders of modern magic." Salem shook his head. "Not even the ancient arts are immune to upgrades or Paramount ratings."

"Cool!"

The fact that the next page remained blank was vaguely disturbing, but Sabrina was too intent on adding shields to her growing stock of absolutely essential spells to worry about it.

"Good morning!" The lilt in Sabrina's voice matched the energetic bounce in her step.

Sitting at the kitchen table, Zelda looked up from the morning newspaper and frowned uncertainly. "Good morning."

"How do I look?" Sabrina twirled for inspection. The conditioner had done an admirable job of restoring the softness and shine to her hair, and she wore it clipped back at the base of her neck in a wood-grained barrette. Inspired by the fashions depicted in a recent teen magazine, she had wished up a short, light-brown flared skirt, laced brown shoes with stubby two-inch heels, and a sky blue Shaker sweater worn over a white knit shirt. Plain gold stud earrings and a single-strand gold chain necklace completed the outfit.

"Honestly?" Zelda raised an eyebrow. "You look a little like Marcia from *The Brady Bunch.*"

Sabrina beamed. "Great! Everything from fifties capri pants to platform shoes from the seventies are back in!"

"All at the same time?" Zelda shook her head. "Style or no style, I will never wear a sack dress again."

"Not a problem, Aunt Zelda. Not unless they bring them back and call them something else."

Hilda watched them both with marginal tolerance.

"A sack dress by any other name—"

"—is still a sack dress." Sabrina wrinkled her nose and shuddered. "Too creepy to contemplate."

"You're certainly feeling chipper this morning, Sabrina—for someone living under a cloud of doom." Setting a bag of flour down on the island counter, Hilda glanced at the hidden pantry where they kept their spell ingredients. "You didn't help yourself to a dose of jolly ginger juice, did you?"

"Or a sprinkle of happy hog-tooth powder?" Zelda looked at Sabrina askance.

"Nope." Bubbling over with euphoric glee, Sabrina slid into a chair and clasped her hands on the table. Both aunts gazed at her a moment, then looked at each other with puzzled concern.

"Where's Tanya?" Hilda asked suddenly and sharply.

Aunt Zelda's head snapped back around. "You didn't put some nasty creepy-crawly spell on her, did you?"

"Not that she doesn't deserve it," Hilda muttered as she picked up an egg and cracked it on the rim of the bowl.

"No. She's still asleep. I wanted to test my shield spell first, before I tackle Tanya on her own terms," Sabrina explained excitedly. "To make sure it works."

Zelda grinned. "You got the book to give you shields! That's wonderful."

"Stupid book. I really wish Drell hadn't done that alternate command edit." Pointing the eggshell into the trash, Hilda levitated a measuring cup and zipped it toward the sink. "All that futuristic mumbo jumbo gives me a headache."

"I think it's called technobabble," Sabrina said.

"Whatever." Filling the cup with water, Hilda pointed it back and dumped the water in the bowl. "I'll stick with good, old-fashioned nonsense rhymes and gibberish, thank you very much." She began to stir with an agitated passion.

"What are you doing, Aunt Hilda?" Sabrina asked.

"Making pancakes."

"But you're using a spoon and regular stuff."

"Only to prove to Zelda that you can't tell the difference between pointed pancakes and pancakes made from scratch."

"There's a difference," Zelda said emphatically.

"Speaking of scratch—" Salem paused in the doorway to stretch and yawn, then jumped into Zelda's lap. "I could use one right between the ears."

"And I could use some help," Sabrina said. "Somebody's got to throw a spell at me so I can test my shield."

"I don't think so." Hilda pointed at the spoon, setting it to self-stir, then rubbed her aching arm.

Aunt Zelda sighed. "We can't do that, Sabrina. If your shield *does* work, and I'm sure it does, whatever spell we cast will come back on us."

"And let's not forget that shield spells don't last indefinitely," Hilda added. "In some cases, they're totally useless."

Sabrina paled. "Define *indefinitely*. What cases?"

"It takes energy and experience to keep a shield up and functioning effectively," Hilda explained. "How long they last depends on a lot of variables which are too complex to go into right now. But if I had to guess, I'd say one of your shields could stay potent for half an hour. Forty-five minutes, tops—if all conditions are ideal."

"And then?" Sabrina sighed. All these qualifiers had to be part of the text from the still-blank page in her book. Fortunately, Aunt Hilda didn't have any qualms about supplying the missing information. In fact, she was being oddly discouraging. Sabrina tucked that piece of trivia away for future reference.

"And then you have to wait until your system recharges before you can raise another one," Zelda said. "How long that takes is another variable. Could be anywhere from five minutes to an hour."

"Maybe longer," Hilda added.

Sabrina nodded. "So when *don't* they work?"

"Usually it's because a witch is taken by surprise," Zelda said. "And although we don't like to admit it, some witches *are* more powerful than others."

"Two or more witches working together against a single witch are pretty good at shield-busting, too. That's given Zelda and me an advantage on numerous occasions."

"Okay, but none of those things are relevant to my problem now, and I really need to know if my shield works!" Desperate, Sabrina tried a little anxious pleading. "You don't have to do anything gross or terrible. Just a simple harmless spell will be fine. Please. My confidence is practically bottomed out as it is. If I'm not sure—"

"Oh, all right." Throwing up her hands, Hilda took a deep breath and raised her finger.

"Careful, Hilda," Zelda warned.

Nodding, Hilda glanced around the kitchen, then focused on the open bag of flour. "Flour powder, soft and white, into Sabrina's face take flight!"

She pointed.

"Fire!" Salem ducked.

A stream of white powder exploded out of the flour bag, headed toward Sabrina.

Zelda winced.

Sabrina threw up a protective arm.

The stream of flour suddenly executed a one-hundred-and-eighty-degree turn and collided with Hilda's face in a billowing puff of white dust. Blinking the powder out of her eyes, Hilda grinned. "It works."

"Yes!" Leaping out of her chair, Sabrina grabbed her crocheted shoulder bag and ran for the door. "Gotta go to work! This is so cool!" She paused at the door and looked back. "And if Tanya wants to know where I am, you can tell her. A healthy dose of her own medicine is definitely in order. I can't *wait* to even up the score!"

"Sabrina—" Salem fell out of Zelda's lap as she stood up.

"What?"

"Nothing." Smiling weakly, Zelda sat back down.

Humming, Salem began to groom himself.

"Have fun." Hilda stared at the spoon as it obediently moved through the batter. "You missed a lump." The spoon swished back and forth, crushing the offending clump of unmixed flour against the side of the bowl.

" 'Bye." Unsettled by everyone's sudden reticence, Sabrina eased out the door. Obviously, there was another, mysterious and secret something that no one was willing or able to discuss. The balloon of elation that had lifted her spirits after she mastered the shield spell quickly deflated. Sometimes it seemed like every spell or potion she tried had some horrendous hidden consequence she hadn't considered.

What kind of dreadful catastrophe am I headed for now?

Letting the spoon rest, Hilda sat down beside Zelda. "It's out of our hands, you know."

Zelda nodded. "I know. This wouldn't be a true test if Sabrina knew the answers. But that doesn't make me feel a whole lot better."

Sighing, Hilda waved her hand. Instantly clean and dry, the batter bowl and wooden spoon vanished back into their proper places in the cabinet. A steaming plate of pancakes with melting butter and warm maple syrup appeared in front of her. "I always get hungry when I worry, and I'm too worried to cook."

"I'm too worried to eat," Zelda said.

"But I can't say I'd blame Sabrina for trying to get a little revenge after the way Tanya's treated her." Suddenly losing her appetite, Hilda shoved the plate aside and glanced up toward the room where Tanya was still sleeping. Ever since the Witch Wars of 7620 O.R., young witches and warlocks had been unknowingly subjected to a required pass-or-fail test of character. It was necessary to weed out and teach the truly incorrigible a solid lesson before they did too much damage.

"Hmmm," Zelda agreed. "The only thing that's saved Tanya so far is that Sabrina didn't know about shields."

"And now she does. Maybe just being able to protect herself from Tanya will be enough to satisfy her," Hilda offered hopefully. "I didn't feel cheated when Cousin Jeffrey's spell bounced off us and he was stuck being a horse for a hundred years. Did you?"

"Not at all." Zelda smiled. "Especially since he was stuck being a mare."

"See? There *is* justice!" Hilda grinned.

The brief sparkle that flickered in Zelda's eyes faded. "That's the problem, though, isn't it? Justice. Sabrina doesn't know her shield won't protect her from her own spells. Of course, maybe Tanya doesn't know that, either."

"They could both fail," Hilda observed. "It's happened before."

"Yes, but so far, Sabrina apparently hasn't cast any spells with lasting effects that can't be fixed. But what if—" Zelda shook her head quickly. "No. That's just too gruesome to imagine."

"Aren't you two selling Sabrina a little short?" Salem asked. "You're assuming she's going to fail."

"Not necessarily." Pulling the plate back, Hilda warmed up the pancakes with a sizzling point. "It's just that if she passes, there's no problem. If she fails—"

"Big problem—maybe." Zapping herself a fork, Zelda helped herself to a bite of Hilda's pancakes.

"Possibly." Hilda fixed Salem with a grave look of warning. "So until we know how this whole thing turns out, don't chase down and devour any delectable-looking critters you find running around the house, okay?"

"I promise," the cat said solemnly. "But it won't be easy."

"I really hope Sabrina doesn't come home as a snake." Zelda shivered with disgust. "I just can't stand feeding live mice to reptiles."

"That won't bother me," Hilda said matter-of-factly. "But if she turns herself into a toad, taking care of her will be your responsibility, Zelda. That includes catching the flies. I haven't had a wart in five hundred years and it takes me decades to get rid of them."

"Deal."

"Well, *if* the worst happens, I'm kind of hoping for the snake." Salem purred thoughtfully. "A ready supply of live mice sounds good to me."

Hilda scowled—fondly. The perversity of cats was almost charming. Her heart skipped a beat when a rustling drew her attention to the door. "Hello, Tanya. How long have you been standing there?"

"Long enough." Tanya smiled.

☆

Chapter 9

☆

Tanya was relegated to the back of Sabrina's mind by the time she reached the mall. There was no way the girl could take her by surprise again, and even with a limited time period, her shield would protect her against any more embarrassing afflictions. Besides, there was one unwritten rule of conduct that most witches, with the exception of Aunt Vesta, seemed to respect. Witches did not deliberately draw attention to themselves or their magical powers by causing major inexplicable disturbances in public. So far, even Tanya had restricted herself to irritating, but not too remarkable pranks, which would work in Sabrina's favor at the busy mall.

Feeling calm and confident, Sabrina marched

into Too Chic Boutique at nine-fifty, ready and eager to go to work.

"Very attractive, Sabrina!" Aubrey Holcomb closed the cash register drawer and eyed her with relieved approval. The manager was looking fashionably hot in belted, dark brown, flared pants and a long-sleeved, light green blouse with a dramatically tapered collar. A scarf with a swirling pattern in shades of the same colors was loosely knotted around her neck, and brown platform shoes easily added three inches to her height.

"Just something I threw together." Sabrina smiled and set her purse behind the counter. "So where do I start?"

"Why don't you just familiarize yourself with what's in the store so you won't be completely lost when we open. Then I'll show you how to ring up a purchase. To be honest, it's been an extremely slow month and I'm hoping for a really good day. And I, uh—don't want you to get so nervous you start stuttering again. No offense."

"None taken and no problem. I'll be fine. Yesterday I was just worried that I wouldn't get the job. But I did, so now I'm not worried and so—I won't stutter." Taking a deep breath, Sabrina started down the center aisle. "I'll just look around."

"Oh, wait." Aubrey reached into a shelf under the curved counter and pulled out a black badge with Sabrina's name printed on it in gold. "I thought you might like to have this. It helps if the customers can identify the people who work here."

"Thanks." Pinning the badge onto her sweater, Sabrina felt her spirits soar again. Despite their rocky start the day before, Aubrey was graciously trying to make her feel at ease. The gesture was greatly appreciated. *And,* Sabrina thought as she strolled through the elegant and immaculate store, *I have a feeling Too Chic Boutique sales are going to be fantastic today!*

As the first idle browsers began to wander in, Sabrina didn't waste any time putting her magical sales expertise into action. Rather than taking the spell off the mirror she had enchanted for Jocelyn's benefit the previous afternoon, she made certain every mirror in the store produced the same effect. After that, it was merely a question of making sure everyone found exactly what they were looking for.

"What size?" Sabrina asked a husky young woman who was trying to decide between a skirt or slacks to go with the jacket she liked.

Pretty and impeccably groomed despite her chunky figure, the woman avoided Sabrina's gaze when she answered, "Nine. Definitely a nine."

The woman could probably squeeze into a nine, but she wore a size eleven. However, Sabrina wasn't about to argue the point. Disagreeing would only upset the customer and ruin a potential sale.

"I'm sure we have a nine in that color." Turning her back to the woman, Sabrina pulled a skirt and a pair of slacks off the rack. With a quick point, she changed the size-eleven tags into nines. "Here. Why don't you try both? If you like them, you'd have more options for wearing the jacket. We've even got some scoop-neck tees in complementary colors that would just look dynamite with these, too."

After loading the woman down with things to try on, Sabrina escorted her to the fitting room. Aubrey was at the cash register ringing up a leather bag. Sabrina had changed the shade ever so slightly to fit the fussy customer's specifications. She was almost sure these subtle touches of magic didn't count as mortal meddling. Her spells were just an innovative marketing technique.

"I've never shopped in here before," the woman at the cash register said, "but I *will* be back. I never thought I'd find a purse to match this suit."

Catching Sabrina's eye, Aubrey winked.

Grinning, Sabrina turned to watch a teenaged girl shifting from one foot to the other in front of Jocelyn's mirror. She had on a shimmering silver dress cut in simple, flowing lines. Blond and blue-eyed with perfect skin, she also had the figure and legs to wear the skimpy shift.

"I just *love* the way this dress looks! It's, like,

totally awesome," the girl gushed, then frowned. "Except I don't think it's quite short enough, do you?" She swiveled to look at Sabrina.

Holding the girl's gaze, Sabrina pointed at the hemline of the dress, shortening it by two inches. "I'm not sure you'd want it much shorter."

Shrugging, the girl turned back to the mirror and blinked. "You know, you're right. I could have sworn it was too long, but it's not, is it? Ragin'." Thrilled, the girl continued to admire herself in the enchanted mirror.

The husky woman came out of the fitting room flushed with delight. "It's so hard for me to find clothes that fit right. But these are absolutely stunning. Would you take them to the counter for me? I'm going to look around some more."

"Sure." Draping the jacket, slacks, skirt, and two tees over her arm, Sabrina sighed. She didn't wonder that the woman never found anything that fit, not if she was stubbornly trying on nines when she obviously wore elevens. On a roll and anxious to see that the pleasant customer went home with a wardrobe that was properly sized, Sabrina rushed to the cash register to drop off the clothes.

Aubrey was beaming. "If this keeps up, we're going to break our all-time Saturday sales record before three!"

"Really? What time is it now?"

"Almost noon." Aubrey spied the teenager

coming out of the fitting room with the silver dress. "Is she going to take that?"

"I'll be real surprised if she doesn't," Sabrina said.

"Great! It's from the fall collection and I thought I'd never get rid of it because of the price. It's still over a hundred dollars on clearance!" Forgetting her studied cool and reserved demeanor, Aubrey laughed and jiggled with excitement. "I do believe you're charmed, Sabrina."

"Could be," Sabrina quipped as she hurried away to find the wandering size eleven. Although Sabrina now knew how to ring up a sale, Aubrey clearly preferred to work the register and leave Sabrina on the sales floor. The morning had gone quickly and infinitely better than Sabrina had thought possible. The day and her mood improved by megaleaps as she walked down the aisle in front of the window and saw Libby peering in.

The cheerleader glared at Sabrina with a dark and fuming expression that was uniquely her own. If looks had the power to reduce people to puddles of quivering jelly, Sabrina would have been oozing all over the floor. Fortunately, Libby's power was limited to the force of her intimidating personality and caustic words, which could only reduce people to human semblances of quivering jelly.

Immune and amused, Sabrina waved.

Defiantly lifting her chin, Libby turned and stalked away.

Just too cool! Sabrina thought as she spotted the attractive, heavyset woman flipping through a rack of designer jeans.

Jenny caught up to Sabrina before she reached the target customer. "Can you get away for lunch?"

"I don't know." Sabrina frowned as two more customers walked in. "It's so busy."

"Ask anyway," Jenny insisted. "I *really* want to 'do lunch,' and Harvey's gonna meet us at Hong Kong to Go in five minutes."

"He is?" Sabrina sighed. "Okay, I'll see what I can do. Wait for me by the fountain."

"Great. See ya in a few minutes."

As Jenny dashed off, Sabrina turned her attention back to the size eleven, wondering how to cope with the woman's problem. A spell was the only logical solution. With a discreet point, Sabrina mumbled an impromptu incantation.

"Pick size eleven; see a size nine, and whatever you try will fit you just fine."

Shaking her head slightly, the woman replaced the size-nine jeans she was holding and grabbed an eleven. A huge smile brightened her face as she glanced at the tag. With that problem solved, Sabrina dashed back to the counter where Aubrey had just finished cashing out the girl with the silver dress.

"Would it be all right if I went to lunch now?"

"Now?" Aubrey's eyes narrowed as she scanned the store. "I don't think so, Sabrina. I can't run the register and help all these people, too."

"They don't really look like they need much help," Sabrina observed. And that was the truth, she realized as she looked around. The enchanted mirrors were doing all the work. Two more satisfied customers were heading for the counter with their selections. The only difficulty she could foresee was that Aubrey might not be able to ring the sales up fast enough. *And that's easy to fix,* she thought with a mischievous grin.

Stepping aside so the two women could get to the counter, Sabrina swept her finger over the room.

Patience is as patience does. You don't mind waiting to pay because you just found something else today.

As Aubrey started to scan the tag on the first customer's pants and matching vest, the woman's gaze zeroed in on a rack of lined crocheted tops. "Wait! Just hold these, okay? I have *got* to try on one of those shirts."

"Certainly." Shrugging, Aubrey smiled at the second woman, who took three pairs of earrings off the counter display and added them to her pile.

"Would you like some help?" Sabrina asked the woman charging toward the crocheted shirts.

"No, thanks." She didn't even look at Sabrina as she ran by.

Sabrina did a quick survey of the other shoppers and got the same response. "Everyone seems perfectly content to browse on their own and—it might be even busier later."

Nodding, Aubrey reluctantly relented. "All right, but don't be too long."

"I won't." Grabbing her purse, Sabrina ran for the door.

Jenny jumped up from a stone bench and fell into step beside Sabrina as they wove their way through the Saturday crowd. Excited about her own experience at The Dickens Den, she didn't stop talking until they stepped off the escalator on the second level.

"Then this guy, who is, like, a total hunk with a classic California tan and muscles that were so huge they were bursting through the seams of his shirt, asks for the gourmet cooking section." Jenny's hand went to her chest as she dipped and swayed in a slight swoon. "I just stared at him like a jerk, I was so surprised. I mean, health food or physical fitness, yes, but gourmet cooking? Fortunately, it took me only a few seconds to recover. He was so cool. I felt like I was having a waking dream the whole time I waited on him."

"So what happened?"

"Happened?" Jenny blinked. "He bought two vegetarian cookbooks and left."

"Oh." Shaking her head, Sabrina smiled and waved when she saw Harvey pacing in front of the Chinese takeout. Harvey was not a muscle-bound California vegetarian gourmet, but he was a hunk and he was a dream—come true.

"Hey, Harvey! Hi!"

Jenny tapped Sabrina on the shoulder. "Apparently, your cousin wasn't nearly as annoyed with Libby as she wanted us to think."

"Huh?" Puzzled, Sabrina frowned, then glanced in the direction of Jenny's narrowed gaze. Tanya and Libby were sitting together at a table on the far side of the Food Court, conferring as they watched Harvey.

Sabrina sagged. She had been so preoccupied with the mysterious, though still unconfirmed test, unfrizzing her own hair, worrying about how she could survive Tanya's torment, not to mention staying awake half the night learning about shields and then working all morning, she hadn't dwelled on Tanya's impending trip to the movies with Harvey. The situation was annoying, but hardly threatened her and Harvey's relationship. Although Tanya had manipulated the invitation, love spells, charms, and potions weren't possible. And Sabrina trusted Harvey completely.

The fact that Tanya was three hours early and having lunch with Libby was a bit unsettling, though. As both girls turned and fastened their stone-cold gazes on her and Jenny, Sabrina raised her shield. A tickling sensation that felt like every downy hair had suddenly been charged with static electricity washed over her skin.

"Like two peas in a pod," Sabrina muttered as she steered Jenny toward Hong Kong to Go around the opposite side of the large seating area.

"Libby and Tanya?" Jenny nodded. "I know this is going to sound strange, Sabrina, but I got the distinct impression that Tanya had something to do with your hair going all weird last night."

"Yeah, well—she did." *Think fast, Sabrina!* "She, uh—put this flyaway hair stuff in my shampoo and the, uh—active ingredients are— time-released! So the effect doesn't happen right away."

"What a despicable thing to do to your own cousin." Jenny exhaled with disgust.

"It runs in her branch of the family," Sabrina explained. "Her father used to pull the same kind of stuff on my aunts."

"Come on. I'm starving." Waving them to hurry, Harvey moved back so Sabrina and Jenny could get in line ahead of him. "Working's a lot more fun than I thought it would be, but it sure does build up an appetite."

"You build up an appetite when you're asleep, Harvey," Sabrina teased.

"You're right." Harvey grinned sheepishly. "I wake up famished every morning."

"So you're enjoying The Sports Palace?" Jenny asked while they waited for their orders at the pickup counter.

"Yeah. It's not hard at all. All I have to do is show people where stuff is and demonstrate how it works. I may take up golf."

"Golf?" Grabbing her tray, Sabrina looked at Harvey askance.

"Never thought I'd like it. But after trying out a few clubs this morning on the indoor putting green, I realized there's a lot more to it than hitting a ball around a field." Loading his own tray with soy sauce and hot mustard packets, Harvey turned to lead them to a table. "Besides, dentists are a lot like doctors. Golf would be a good thing to—"

Harvey suddenly rocked back on his heels as though he'd been punched in the stomach.

Sabrina instantly looked across the room. Tanya was pointing at the stricken boy. Her smile tightened as she executed another exaggerated point. Sitting beside her, Libby gasped with surprise.

Harvey stumbled forward, tipping his tray. The plate heaped with chow mein, orange chicken, fried rice, and two egg rolls slid off and landed upside down on the floor. The large paper cup filled to the brim with orange soda started to topple, then changed directions and spilled off the side, drenching the sleeve of Jenny's blouse.

"Oh, no!" Reacting spontaneously, although

too late to avoid the soda, Jenny jumped back. She stepped on a man's foot.

Untouched and gripping her tray, Sabrina watched in helpless horror as a runaway chain reaction of accidents followed within the space of a few seconds.

The man reached out to push Jenny off his foot and flipped *his* tray, which was stacked with burgers, fries, and milk shakes. The wrapped sandwiches and boxed fries went flying backward, pelting three preteen boys. The milk shakes bombed the floor behind the man, splattering his trousers as the tops popped off on landing.

Jenny staggered forward and whirled in a stunned daze, whacking a passing woman with her elbow. Sabrina managed a quick point to stabilize the food on Jenny's tray, preventing her friend's lunch from becoming more inedible garbage on the floor. However, everything else was happening too fast to make damage control even remotely possible.

The elbowed woman shrieked and turned, smacking with her heavy purse a gray-haired custodian removing a trash bag from a refuse container. Unbalanced, the man fell headfirst into the empty trash bin.

Arm cocked to throw one of the burger grenades back, a furious preteen boy lunged at the sore-foot man. The boy slipped on the gooey glob of spilled milk shakes, fell, and slid an unbelievable twelve feet into a gaggle of giggling junior-high girls, sending them running and squealing for safety.

"Over here!" Sabrina hissed at Harvey and Jenny, motioning them away from the mess as a security guard rushed to the scene. Herding them to a table, Sabrina watched as the uniformed man hauled the boy with the milk shake–smeared jeans to his feet. The boy pulled loose from the guard's grip and shrugged when questioned. The burger bomber with the stomped-on foot began to scan the court.

Looking for us, no doubt. Sabrina focused her finger.

"Out of sight, out of mind . . ." Drawing a blank, she pointed and hoped the partial incantation would be good enough. It was. The man shook his head, sighed, and stormed toward the exit. The elbowed woman was long gone, along with the screeching girls. The custodian had freed himself from the trash bin with no apparent ill effects beyond embarrassed bewilderment.

Confident that they wouldn't be implicated in the food-fumbling incident, which might have resulted in being banned from the mall, Sabrina looked at Harvey and Jenny.

Crestfallen, Harvey stared at his empty tray.

Jenny stared at the soaked fabric clinging to her arm in wide-eyed disbelief.

The sound of muffled giggling rose above the drone of conversation in the Food Court, distracting Sabrina from her friends' problems. She turned to see Tanya and Libby desperately trying to control themselves. Both girls lost it, doubling over in fits of laughter. Meeting Sabrina's angry gaze, Tanya held up her finger and blew on it, as though it were a smoking gun.

Sabrina seethed. Knowing her shield protected her from Tanya's magic, she hadn't stopped to consider that her arrogant cousin might try to get to her through her friends. The concept was too deviously mean-spirited to have entered her mind. Tanya didn't care that her spiteful prank had caused harm and humiliation to a horde of innocent bystanders, either. Believing herself to be superior, she regarded mortals as inconsequential objects of amusement unworthy of her lofty concern.

But Tanya was in for an eye-opening, attitude-adjusting shock. Mortals were powerless to combat her unmerciful magic, but Sabrina was not.

Spotting four husky players from the Westbridge High football team walking toward Tanya and Libby's table with trays full of pizza, ice cream, and sodas, Sabrina flexed her finger. The chance to retaliate for Tanya's atrocious behavior was too inviting to resist. And Libby was an eager accomplice. Dumping food into the girls' deserving laps would hardly begin to settle the score, but it was an appropriate start.

Sabrina's shield had been in place for less than ten minutes and was still operating at full capacity.

She raised her finger.

Ready, aim . . .

Chapter 10

A nagging thought triggered an alarm in Sabrina's mind. She quickly curled her potent finger into her fist before releasing the spell. She wasn't sure why.

Maybe it was because Tanya's self-assured gaze had not wavered, as if she was daring her half-mortal cousin to try using her inferior magic against her. With her shield spell functioning, Sabrina's spell would simply bounce off anyway.

What would happen then?

Sabrina wondered, remembering the discouraging discussion about the limitations of shields at the breakfast table. Was Aunt Hilda's doom-and-gloom attitude a subtle warning? Everybody *had* seemed oddly withdrawn when she left for the mall, as though they wanted to say something but didn't dare. Perhaps there was more information missing from the ominous blank page in her book than she realized.

Sabrina gasped softly. In her brief experience as a witch, the one lesson she had been exposed to over and over again was that using magic without considering all the possible ramifications was dangerous.

What if her own shield wouldn't protect her from her own spell when it bounced off *Tanya's* shield?

Sabrina didn't know if that assumption was correct, and she wasn't about to cast a spell on a shielded witch to find out. However, she realized with a flash of insight, an experiment to prove the theory wasn't necessary. Tanya's fatal finger had avoided her during the food fiasco. Why? Sabrina sighed. There was only one logical reason. Tanya knew she had learned how to conjure a shield and that any spell she cast would rebound back on her.

Stalemate.

"What am I going to do, Sabrina?" Jenny whined. "I can't go back to the bookstore with a wet sleeve!"

"Cold water," Sabrina suggested quickly, reaching for Jenny's tray. "I'll get this. If you don't take care of that stain right away, it won't come out."

Jenny didn't know it, but her soda-drenched blouse was the least of her troubles. Sabrina had to get her distraught friend out of the immediate area before Tanya got bored and sprang back into action again. Harvey, too.

"Can't hurt to try, I guess." Plucking at the damp material, Jenny sighed and trudged off to the restroom.

"I've got to get something else to eat." Harvey sighed, resigned to the extra expense and delay. "I'll be right back."

"Take your time!" Sabrina called after him as he headed back to Hong Kong to Go. Setting Jenny's tray down, she absently flashed a finger at the retreating girl, removing the orange stain and drying the sleeve. Her thoughts were on Tanya and the frustration of not being able to fix her as easily. Evenly matched in power and both using shields, they had reached an impasse.

Although Sabrina regretted not being able to fight back, she really didn't want to stoop to Libby and Tanya's level, which was pretty low. Knowing she couldn't attack Sabrina without risk to herself, Tanya wouldn't hesitate to torment her friends instead.

Picking up Jenny's tray, Sabrina went looking for a more secluded table. As she passed a frazzled mother, one of the woman's small boys pulled his straw back to flick milk at his younger brother. The straw snapped out of his grasp, spraying the white liquid in his own face instead.

Sabrina stopped dead in her tracks as inspiration struck. Grinning, she whirled and marched across the Food Court toward Tanya and Libby's table.

Sitting at the table next to the two girls, Sabrina casually checked her watch. Her shield was good for only another fifteen to thirty minutes, and she had no way of knowing exactly when it would wear off. Tanya's shield, on the other hand, would last ten minutes longer than hers because Tanya hadn't raised it until after the food follies, when Sabrina had almost made the mistake of pointing back.

"Well, well," Tanya said. As usual, every detail of her appearance was flawless. Shimmering waves of dark hair streamed down her back in stark contrast to the glistening white of a silk shirt. The tapered collar was uncreased and the top three pearl buttons had been daringly left undone. An elaborately hand-tooled leather belt circled her trim waist through the loops of form-fitting jeans. "If it isn't Sabrina, the good witch of the north. How are all your clumsy little munchkin friends doing?"

Clumsy munchkins! Sparks of outrage flared in Sabrina's mind. Outwardly, she ignored the cruel remark.

"Witch is right." Libby scowled, her misguided anger about Too Chic Boutique overriding her twisted sense of humor. "I want my job back!"

Slipping her chopsticks out of a paper wrapper, Sabrina glanced at Libby with feigned innocence. The cheerleader was wearing a stunning loosely knit beige vest over a stylish light blue blouse tucked into a short, dark blue skirt. With her stubby-heeled shoes and elegantly simple gold earrings, she looked a bit overdressed for a day at a hobby and game store. "What happened? Did you get fired from Toy Town already?"

"You know what I mean!" Libby snapped.

"You're right. I do. I saw the black mark you put on the Too Chic slip." Smiling, Sabrina deftly clamped the chopsticks around a chunk of beef.

Libby rose and leaned over the table, her low voice full of menace. "Are you calling me a *cheat?*"

"I think we're looking at the cheat, Libby." Tanya placed her hand on Libby's arm to calm her, but her icy blue eyes were riveted on Sabrina. "You stole Libby's job, Sabrina, and I intend to make sure she gets it back."

Chewing slowly, Sabrina nodded and swallowed. "Really? And just how do you plan to do that?"

Tanya rolled her eyes. "I have it on good authority that some"—she glanced at Libby cautiously—"*people* are more powerful than others."

Libby nodded in complete agreement.

Sabrina hardly dared breathe. *What* good authority? Had Cousin Jeffrey told Tanya about shields and their limitations? Or had she figured it out for herself? It was even possible Tanya had overheard the conversation with her aunts this morning. Sabrina wondered, but realized it didn't really matter. The only thing that mattered now was Tanya's unshakable belief that she *was* more powerful.

And the hope that she wasn't!

Baiting the trap, Sabrina faked an expression of uncertain fear.

"I don't think the manager of Too Chic Boutique will want you to stay when you go back to work looking like a total scuz." A scheming sparkle gleamed in Tanya's eyes as she started speaking in a rhythmic cadence. "Shield dissolve and witch beware . . . tangles and frizzies and flyaway hair!" She pointed.

Blinking in disbelief, Libby turned to look at the chanting girl as though Tanya had gone totally over the edge.

Sabrina felt the *ping* of a slight vibration.

Still pointing, Tanya crooned, "Tattered and torn, dirty and worn, your wardrobe poor and strictly thrift store!"

Libby's hand flew to her mouth to stifle a cry of stupefied awe.

With difficulty, Sabrina maintained an exterior calm. Inside she was jumping up and down with exuberant excitement as Tanya's long, luxurious hair sizzled and fried into a dark mass of tangles, split ends, and frizzies. Instead of a silk shirt and designer jeans, she was suddenly wearing a grungy white T-shirt. The collar seam was split and the ripped pocket of the plaid work shirt she had on over the tee flopped open. Knotted clothesline rope belted faded, torn, and dirt-smeared jeans that were two sizes too big.

"This is just too weird!" Libby's chair fell over as she jumped out of it. "You hypnotized me with all that hocus-pocus stuff, right? That's it, right?" Holding her hands out as though to ward off a contagious disease, Libby backed away from Tanya and the table. "Oh, who cares? I'm gone!"

Neither Sabrina nor Tanya broke the locked stare connecting them, to watch Libby run for the escalator. Sabrina knew she could count on only seven or eight more minutes of protection from her shield spell. If she was going to beat Tanya at her own game, she had to do it fast.

"Why didn't my spell work?" Tanya demanded.

"It did." Sabrina struggled not to smile as Tanya frowned with perplexed consternation. Anchored in denial, the girl either hadn't heard or stubbornly refused to accept the implication of Sabrina's comment. Unaware of the dramatic change in her appearance, Tanya tried again.

"Chair of sturdy wooden leg, shatter like a broken egg." Concentrating, Tanya pointed.

Sabrina gripped the table. She was shielded, but the chair she was sitting on wasn't. However, the spell shield apparently extended beyond her own person to include whatever she was touching.

A shriek erupted from Tanya as her chair collapsed underneath her. Sprawled on the floor with her hands braced behind her, she blinked in stunned surprise.

The elderly custodian dropped his broom and hurried over. "Are you all right, miss?"

"Get away from me!" Tanya snapped, slapping his extended hand away.

"Don't sue. You won't win." Huffing indignantly, the man left.

"Charming old coot," Tanya muttered. As she started to rise, her gaze settled on the torn knees of the ragged, baggy jeans. Sitting bolt upright, she violently shook her head as her hands patted and probed her altered clothes and finger-fried hair, confirming that her eyes were not playing nasty tricks. Another shriek escaped her, but this time it was a cry of undiluted rage. Springing to her feet, Tanya stomped to Sabrina's table and leveled her finger at Sabrina's nose. Her body stiffened with the force of her fury. Even the air around her seemed agitated and disturbed.

"Careful where you point that thing," Sabrina cautioned. She gently pushed Tanya's finger aside. "It might go off. And the results aren't pleasant, are they?"

Tanya hesitated. Setting her mouth in a firm line, she straightened into a more dignified posture. Keeping a defiant eye on Sabrina, she raised her hand. "Magic spell that went astray, undo the harm invoked today!" Tanya pointed at herself, took a deep breath, then looked down. Her confident calm exploded into a raving fit of temper when she realized her counterspell hadn't worked.

Sabrina shrank down in her chair, not from fear of Tanya, but because the girl's tantrum was attracting the revolted attention of everyone else in the Food Court. The unkempt tangle of long dark hair and rag-barrel hobo look didn't do a whole lot to dispel the image of crazed derelict, either.

"Fix my clothes and my hair right now, Sabrina Spellman! Because if you don't, I'll make you sorry you were ever born! I'll make your friends sorry *they* were ever born, too! Do you understand me? I am *not* kidding!"

"I can't," Sabrina said honestly. "It wasn't my spell that frizzed your hair and changed your clothes. You did it and I can't undo it."

"I can't go around looking like this!" Tanya's threatening tone changed to a desperate plea laced with a pinch of demand. "You must have some idea what to do!"

"Well, actually, yes." Realizing that her shield was on the verge of disintegrating, Sabrina hastened to diffuse Tanya's anger. She graciously offered the only advice she could, based on her own experience. "You can go home and change into some of my clothes. And a whole bottle of superprotein conditioner will get rid of the frizzed snarls in your hair. It takes a while, though."

"Very funny. You really expect me to believe that? I'm not stupid!" Tanya spat out the words. "You'd say or do anything to ruin my date with Harvey at three—"

"Date? What date? You invited yourself!"

Tanya shrugged. "That's totally beside the point."

No, it's not. Sabrina fumed as she reevaluated the situation. Harvey was just being nice when he had agreed to take her visiting cousin to the movies, but he was nothing but a trophy to Tanya. Last night the mute spell had made it impossible for her to object, and complaining to Harvey about it now, without being able to explain the real reasons why, would seem petty and mean. But after the heartless way Tanya had treated Harvey in the Food Court, Sabrina *would* do anything to prevent the meeting—to protect him, not because she wanted to win the pointless contest Tanya was determined to wage. Oddly enough, Tanya's own spiteful nature had saved her the trouble.

"Now, are you going to tell me how to rectify this mess or not?" Tanya yanked her brittle, snarled hair.

"I did," Sabrina said patiently. "Three hefty doses of conditioner applied over the next several hours will solve your problem."

Too late to make the movie, but oh, well!

Tanya's eyes flashed as she leaned forward and placed her palms on the table. Back in control, she spoke with hushed, venomous intensity. "Make no mistake, Sabrina. I am going to get you for this. I will not be ridiculed or beaten by a half-mortal, vicious little beast like *you!*"

Speechless, Sabrina just stared as Tanya wheeled and headed back into the mall. A shivering rippled across her skin as her shield spell suddenly evaporated.

Slumping in relief, Sabrina checked the time. Twelve thirty-two. The shield had lasted exactly thirty minutes. But that had been long enough and she didn't have to worry about how soon she could erect another one. Defeated for the moment, Tanya was probably on her way back to her aunts' house to hide, sulk, and regroup. Besides, whether she appreciated Sabrina's advice or not, she had no options but to take it.

Unless she wants *to spend the rest of the day dressed in rags with horror hair,* Sabrina thought impishly.

"You are *not* going to believe this!" Jenny smiled broadly as she sat down and pulled her food tray toward her. "My blouse was completely dry when I got to the lounge. And there's not a trace of a stain, either."

"Really? That's great."

"I thought I'd never get through that line again." Swinging his leg over the back of a chair,

Harvey dropped his tray on the table, sat down, and dug in.

Propping her chin in one hand, Sabrina toyed with her uneaten beef and broccoli and watched him fondly. Like Jenny, he didn't have the faintest idea that he had barely escaped a head-on collision with catastrophe.

"Oh, yuck!" Grimacing, Jenny put her plastic fork down. "This is cold. And I've got to be back to the store in twenty minutes."

"Me, too." Ripping open a soy sauce packet with his teeth, Harvey squeezed it onto his rice. "You can have one of my egg rolls, Jenny."

Jenny shook her head.

"I'm pretty sure I can get your own lunch warmed up real fast," Sabrina offered. All she had to do was duck behind one of the supporting pillars and point it hot.

"No, thanks. I'm not hungry anymore." Sighing, Jenny folded her arms on the table. "I was really looking forward to having a friendly, relaxing lunch with you guys. But between Harvey spilling his tray and my blouse getting wet so we had to waste time standing in line and going to the restroom, *this* has been a total disaster. People tossing food all over the place didn't help, either. Not exactly what I had in mind, you know?"

"There's always tomorrow," Sabrina suggested brightly.

"Oh, yeah!" Jenny's grin changed to a startled,

questioning frown as loud screams and shouts suddenly reverberated through the Food Court. "What on earth is going on?"

Sabrina didn't have to guess.

Tanya!

"Gotta go!" Jumping up, Sabrina grabbed her tray and dumped her lunch in the trash bin. Jenny was hard on her heels as she raced to the escalator.

"See ya later!" Harvey's hunger being a higher priority than his curiosity, he opted to stay behind and finish eating.

"Excellent!" Jenny laughed when they reached the second-level railing around the open space under the high dome.

Sabrina groaned as she looked into the plaza below.

The central fountain had gone wild. Jets of water sprayed outward instead of gushing gently upward as the center mechanism spun out of control. Shoppers shrieked and sprang out of the line of fire. Small children whooped with delight as they splashed through the huge puddle forming on the floor. Employees and browsers in nearby stores pressed curious faces against window glass to watch. An alarm blared. The tranquil garden gathering place had turned into a madhouse.

Catching the down escalator, Sabrina scanned the chaos for her berserker cousin. There was no doubt in her mind that Tanya was responsible.

Dead set on winning the war she had instigated, she had taken measures Sabrina couldn't ignore to draw her out. And it had worked, Sabrina realized as she spied Tanya hovering behind a supporting pillar. She couldn't just walk away, leaving Tanya to run amok in the mall. Unwilling to accept defeat, Tanya would continue to create one calamity after another until Sabrina confronted her in a final showdown of power.

Sabrina's breath caught in her throat when Tanya looked up and spotted her gliding slowly toward the lower level.

There was one major problem.

Tanya's shield was still functioning.

And hers wasn't.

Chapter 11

☆

☆

There was no malicious glee in Tanya's gaze as she aimed her finger. Her expression was as coldly calculating as her intent was resolute.

Grabbing Jenny's hand, Sabrina carefully slipped by the man on the step below her and raced down the moving stairs. The only thing that saved them from being instantly zapped by Tanya's imminent spell was a group of sopping wet, laughing teenagers who dashed in front of the girl.

Three of them tripped over their own feet and slid across the slick plaza floor on their stomachs.

They thought it was hilarious.

Sabrina and Jenny might have been critically injured if they had fallen down the escalator.

Hitting the floor running, Sabrina tried to haul

Jenny into the gathering crowd. She didn't harbor any unrealistic hopes that Tanya might think twice before unleashing a dangerous spell on a mob of innocent mortals. She was hoping to lose herself in the throng, buying time until she could conjure another spell shield. Then maybe she'd have a fighting chance of luring Tanya out of the congested mall.

Jenny suddenly pulled free, pausing to watch the spectacular water show. "What's the hurry, Sabrina? We don't have to be back until one, and it's only quarter of."

As Jenny eased into the crowd, Sabrina reached out to grab her shirt and missed. Frantic, she searched the opposite side of the plaza for Tanya.

Moving in front of the pillar, Tanya scanned the mob, too. Her gaze swept right past Sabrina, but a slow smile bloomed on her face as she focused her finger. Having lost track of her adversary, she was apparently willing to settle for the next best thing.

Jenny.

Sabrina shoved her way through the mass of water watchers, reaching Jenny's side just as a tremendous *wooosh* of forced air lifted the startled girl off her feet.

"Sabrina! What's happening?" Jenny cried out as she started to rise. "Do something!"

Although she couldn't counter Tanya's spell, Sabrina thought she might be able to counter the effects. *Air above, downward blow! Equalize the force below.* Snapping her finger, Sabrina held her breath as the downdraft she had conjured negated the force of Tanya's updraft. The people surrounding them were too mesmerized by the berserk fountain to notice the airborne girl slowly dropping back to the ground.

Shaken, Jenny looked at Sabrina with wide, frightened eyes. "Something really strange is going on here!"

"Haven't you ever seen *The Seven Year Itch?*" Latching onto Jenny's arm, Sabrina forced her to follow again. Now that her friend was *the* substitute target for Tanya's vengeful wrath, she had to get her safely out of sight somewhere, too.

"That old movie where Marilyn Monroe stands on the air vent?" Jenny blinked as she scampered behind Sabrina. "Is that what just happened?"

Breaking out of the crowd to the rear, Sabrina nodded. "Probably. Whatever glitch in the system is making the fountain go crazy must have pushed more air through the vent than it was supposed to."

"Cool!"

A quick glance back didn't ease Sabrina's mind. There were so many people in the plaza, she couldn't tell if Tanya was still standing by the distant pillar. At least the tenacious witch wasn't following.

Because she had headed them off at the pass instead!

Spotting Tanya on the concourse in front of them, Sabrina skidded to a halt.

Jenny jerked to a stop beside her. "Now what?"

Sabrina didn't have time to explain.

Chest heaving with fury and exertion, Tanya glared at Sabrina. Her tangled, frizzed hair billowed out from her head like an ominous dark cloud warning of the impending storm as she extended her arm.

Trapped in the open with nowhere to hide, Sabrina's options were severely curtailed. Definitely doomed if she didn't do *something,* she tried to conjure another shield. An almost imperceptible tickling teased her skin, then fizzled abruptly. *Too soon!* Sabrina realized too late. And having used up the energy she had stored since her last shield failed, she had probably caused an additional delay of precious minutes before she could successfully initiate another one.

But Tanya didn't know that!

Shifting her gaze and her finger slightly to the left, Tanya set her magical sight on Jenny again.

Boldly stepping in front of her unsuspecting friend, Sabrina fixed Tanya with *her* challenging gaze and desperately hoped the obsessed witch wouldn't call her bluff.

Tanya instantly fisted her finger and yanked her arm back. Then sneering with frustrated rage, she turned and bolted down the concourse.

"You know," Jenny said, cocking her head slightly, "that girl that's running away? She looks like a grunge version of your cousin."

Breathless with relief, Sabrina just nodded as several maintenance men with jangling toolboxes raced by on their way to fix the fountain.

"Well, looks like most of the excitement's over." Jenny shrugged. "Guess I might as well get back to the store."

Although positive that the excitement was far from over, Sabrina didn't want to discourage Jenny from going back to work. Preventing Tanya from doing any irrevocable damage would be infinitely easier if she wasn't worried about protecting Jenny.

A collective groan of dismay rose from the mob as the water gushing from the fountain gurgled and stopped.

"Yeah, me, too. Catch ya later." Waving, Sabrina skirted the edge of the dispersing crowd toward Too Chic Boutique. She glanced in the window as she ran past.

Looking slightly frazzled but still smiling, Aubrey stood behind the curved counter ringing up sales. A dozen patient customers waited in line, while another dozen meandered up and down the aisles adding to their purchases. None of them were remotely interested in anything going on in the plaza outside.

When Jenny disappeared through the doors of The Dickens Den across the way, Sabrina turned her full attention to Tanya. She didn't have the vaguest idea what she would do when she caught up to her. Without a shield, she couldn't effectively ward off the other witch's magic. And although letting Tanya turn her into something slimy and gross would probably satisfy the girl's hunger for victory, thus saving the mall and its occupants from her destructive spells, it wasn't a solution Sabrina really wanted to consider.

Except as a last resort.

She had just been lucky Tanya didn't realize she was bluffing when she had jumped in front of Jenny.

Which was odd when Sabrina stopped to think about it.

But she couldn't explore any possible explanations right now. A thunderous crash sent her diving for cover behind a bin of soon-to-be-out-of-date vitamins in front of a health food store.

Cautiously peeking around the end of the display, Sabrina spied Tanya standing by a large potted tree, her arm extended toward two kiosks that had smashed into each other. One had overturned, sending earrings, necklaces, rings, and cufflinks clattering across the hard floor. The second was hopelessly crunched on one end. A rack of sample T-shirts with personal photos on the front canted to one side and several photo-imprinted cups had smashed when they fell.

Suddenly, vendors and passers-by scattered as three more of the small stores-on-wheels became mobile and raced toward certain collision at high speed.

Sabrina watched, wishing there was something she could do. Reacting too late to save the lead kiosk from crashing into the crunched one and sustaining a massive dent, she pointed at the third and fourth in quick succession. Powerless to stop them or alter their speed, she succeeded in changing their direction. The third banged into a potted tree, causing only minor damage to itself and none to the heavy pot. The fourth, loaded with wooden crafts, macramé wall hangings, and assorted baskets, was headed toward a section of brick wall between stores.

Until Tanya pointed at an empty bench and sent it plowing into the rolling kiosk. The large, wheeled display swerved and sped straight for the wide automatic doors into The Sports Palace.

Sabrina winced as the doors opened to admit the runaway kiosk, then gasped when she saw Harvey standing directly in its path inside. Paralyzed with shock, he made no effort to jump clear.

No!

Sabrina pointed as the ministore rammed through. "Skinny doors, *por favor!*" It was probably the lamest incantation she had ever come up with, but this *was* an emergency.

And it worked.

Glass shattered and metal screeched as the speeding wagon came to an abrupt halt—wedged in the opening her spell had narrowed.

Baskets and wooden plaques shot out the sides and back end of the crumpled cart as though they'd been flung from a catapult. Shoppers ducked, dropping packages to throw their arms over their heads. One of the football players Sabrina had seen at the Food Court caught a flying basket and threw it to a teammate. The second boy handed off to a third, who cradled the basket in his arm and ran for a touchdown between two potted trees.

Harvey burst out laughing, more from relief than from the macabre humor inherent in unexpected and bizarre circumstances.

Other teens on the concourse whistled and cheered, reacting to an adrenaline rush of thrilling fright.

"That was even better than the chase scene in *Random Revenge!*" The boy grinned, giving no one in particular a thumbs-up four-star rating.

Stunned and perplexed, vendors emerged from doorways to survey the damage in head-shaking silence.

"Think it could have been an earthquake?" one man asked as he picked up two pieces of a broken cup and tried to fit them together.

"Here?" Another vendor shrugged. "Beats me, but I rather doubt it." He brightened and snapped his fingers. "An electromagnetic pulse!"

Shoppers, having survived unharmed, gawked with morbid curiosity.

"Aliens!" an elderly man shouted into his wife's ear.

She cuffed him on the arm and rolled her eyes.

Miraculously, except for the merchandise and kiosks, no one had been hurt and nothing damaged.

And no one even suspected that the dark-haired girl dressed in thrift-store clothes could possibly be guilty.

Ironically, Sabrina thought, *aliens are much more believable than witches.*

Stuffing one hand in the back pocket of her baggy jeans, Tanya strolled nonchalantly through the debris, adding insult to injury. With a casual point, she unhinged the photo T-shirt rack and watched as the hangers slid off. Another point swept the jewelry on the floor to both sides, clearing her path.

Baiting me!

And without a trace of fear for herself.

Sabrina crept out of hiding, her mind reeling with the implications of Tanya's attitude and actions. Tanya had been using shield spells longer than she had.

Maybe a lot longer.

. . . energy and experience . . . one of your

*shield spells could stay potent for half an hour.
Forty-five minutes tops . . .*

Aunt Hilda's words came rushing back,
strongly suggesting that practice increased how
long a shield stayed functional. That would explain why Tanya hadn't cast a spell on her a few
minutes ago. The girl thought her half-mortal
cousin's spell shield was still in effect—because
hers still was!

Hugging the storefronts, Sabrina followed
Tanya as she continued through the mall toward
the far end. She couldn't avoid the inevitable
confrontation, but it didn't seem prudent to rush
in without having as much information as
possible—specifically, the status of Tanya's
shield. Another fifteen minutes had gone by
since Tanya had fled the plaza and, according to
Sabrina's aunts, no spell shield lasted indefinitely.

Stopping in front of the novelty store, Tanya
studied the battery-operated stuffed animals ar-
ranged on a table just inside the entrance.

Ducking behind a large brick planter overflow-
ing with lush concealing foliage in the center of
the concourse, Sabrina breathed in deeply. This
time, an experiment was definitely required. The
spell she cast had to be powerful enough to elicit
a reaction from Tanya if her shield was down,
but not so powerful it would incapacitate *her* if it
bounced back.

Raising her hand, Tanya set all the furry

critters on the table barking, jumping, drum beating, and cymbal clanging out of control. Thoroughly enjoying the effects, she pointed at various other devices on nearby shelves. Rectangular Plexiglas containers that slowly tilted back and forth, causing a thick blue liquid to roll in restful waves, rocked faster. The red gently drifting globs in lava lamps suddenly smashed against the clear sides of their containers and into each other at super speeds. Mechanical novelties beeped, buzzed, gonged, laughed, chattered, and rang, creating a maniacal chorus of discordant sound.

Taking advantage of Tanya's enthralled concentration, Sabrina pointed. *Tiny bolt of lightning lock and zing her with a tiny shock.*

Tanya's shoulders shook with smothered laughter as the store's employees panicked and desperately tried to turn off the gizmos and gadgets.

Sabrina rocked backward slightly as a small electric shock sizzled through her finger.

Feeling the *ping* when the shock spell rebounded off her shield, Tanya looked up, then glanced back.

The plant just above Sabrina's head suddenly wilted and blackened. The plant next to it exploded out of the dirt as the freestanding brick planter wall toppled.

Wishing herself into the card and gift shop behind her, Sabrina flashed out of harm's way a split second before the heavy wall fell. Staying out of sight, she watched Tanya's reflection in the angled window as the girl inspected the fallen wall.

Realizing her quarry wasn't crushed underneath it, the enraged witch stormed down the concourse toppling racks, smashing windows, and shoving shoppers.

Sabrina sagged. Only sheer luck had kept the people who had encountered Tanya's tempestuous magic from bodily harm. And that luck was bound to run out, perhaps sooner than later. She couldn't delay the showdown much longer, not even if the *only* way to stop Tanya meant exposing herself to some unspeakable and disgusting spell. Leaving the store to run after her rampaging cousin, she just hoped she had long enough.

As Sabrina sabotaged and circumvented Tanya's chaotic mischief along the way, using spells that countered the desired effects, a plan began to form in her head. She had two potential weapons at her disposal: a spell shield she might or might not be able to raise in time, and Tanya herself.

But time had suddenly run out, too.

Straight ahead, in a dead-end corner of the mall set back from the exit, Tanya was waiting for her. With her frightful dark hair, blazing blue eyes, and fanatic scowl, she looked like a demented fiend as she slowly raised an arm to point at Sabrina.

A cut from the latest Cranberries CD blared through speakers outside Mad Mike's Music and Video, the only store in the large, isolated alcove.

Since every second might make the difference between success and failure, Sabrina didn't dare try to conjure a spell shield until absolutely necessary. But she couldn't let Tanya know that was a problem, either—not unless she *wanted* to slither, creep, hop, or crawl out of the mall as something other than a teenaged girl.

"You think you're pretty smart, don't you?" Tanya demanded as Sabrina sauntered to an unconcerned stop about ten feet away.

Fixing a look of calm confidence on her smiling face, Sabrina shrugged. Calm hardly described the nervous turmoil in her stomach, but she was on slightly more solid ground in the confidence department. Although her wits hadn't *completely* thwarted Tanya's best efforts to devastate the mall, she had kept her friends, herself, and numerous other people safe.

So far.

"You can't just stomp all over people and get away with it, Tanya." Sabrina had to raise her voice to be heard over the loud music, but she hoped to keep Tanya talking. Locked in verbal combat, Tanya would delay launching another spell. And Sabrina would gain a few more crucial seconds.

"Oh, can't I?" Sneering, Tanya glanced inside the music store and aimed her finger.

Sabrina's head snapped around. Jerry Evans, the budding Nobel prize winner for physics, stood high on a ladder putting a stack of CDs on a shelf. With a quick point, she clamped the ladder to the floor and wall in the same instant Tanya commanded it to fall backward.

Trapped between both magical imperatives, the ladder began to shake violently. Shoving the CDs into place, Jerry scurried to safety on the floor.

A new song suddenly blasted from the store's outside speakers.

"That's it!" Sputtering with rage, Tanya spun on Sabrina. "I have had it with you, Sabrina Spellman! Why don't you just get lost!"

This is *it,* Sabrina thought with a mixture of elation and dread. Tanya was so arrogant and angry, she might forget some of the more fundamental aspects of her magic. At least, that's what Sabrina was counting on.

"What?" Putting a hand to her ear, Sabrina pretended not to be able to hear. Before her aunts had taught her the simple wishing spell, she had turned baby Rudy Gerson into a two-hundred-pound, fifty-year-old version of himself. She had fondly referred to the wishing technique as the Mr. Kazootie spell ever since.

She hoped Tanya wanted to get rid of her as much as she had wanted Rudy to go to sleep so she could spend time with Harvey.

If so, all she had to do to conquer Tanya was

provoke the girl into repeating her wish three times.

And get her spell shield up and running.

"You heard me!"

Shaking her head, Sabrina held her hands out palms up and shrugged to indicate that she had not heard. Inside, she drew on every ounce of energy she had to conjure the shield.

"Get lost!" Tanya yelled.

Not even a snap, crackle, or pop! Alarmed, Sabrina focused, forcing herself to concentrate. If her shield didn't come up before Tanya screamed her wish the third time, there was no telling *where* she'd be lost, or for how long!

Raising her fists in a fit of fury, Tanya stamped her feet. "Get lost! Get—"

An electrified tickling swept over Sabrina's skin, surrounding her in the invisible protective power of the spell shield.

"—lost!"

Sabrina tensed, holding her breath for the few seconds it always took for the Mr. Kazootie spell to take effect. It had been so close, she didn't know if she had conjured the shield in the nick of time.

Or if Tanya had uttered that final fateful word first.

Chapter 12

Ping!

Sensing the slight vibration as Tanya's wish bounced off her shield, Sabrina started to sigh. The air stalled in her lungs as she met Tanya's smug, chilling stare.

Their gazes locked for a split second that seemed like an eternity.

Then, realizing something was wrong, Tanya's ferocious scowl shifted into a frown of uncertainty. Suddenly aware of what she had done, she shook her head in rigorous denial. Eyes wide with terror, she started to shriek—and vanished.

Sabrina blinked.

Tanya was gone—not with a deafening boom of thunder and a blinding flash of light, but in a puff of pink smoke that had popped ever so slightly.

Now what?

Sabrina waited, casting a wary glance around the alcove. Would the Witch's Council hold her accountable for Tanya's unknown fate?

Seconds passed.

Nothing happened.

Apparently not!

In retrospect, Sabrina realized that wasn't surprising. Determined to win in a senseless contest of power she had provoked and escalated, Tanya alone was responsible for whatever destiny she had inadvertently wished herself into.

Feeling a little dizzy as her adrenaline levels dropped, Sabrina sank onto a bench near the mall exit. She relaxed, allowing herself the luxury of taking several deep, calming breaths without having to worry about what diabolical prank her cousin was going to pull next.

Tanya was gone, lost in an unknown somewhere Sabrina didn't care to contemplate. With luck, the girl would stay gone for a long, long time. Sabrina didn't want to think about Tanya's cataclysmic potential for revenge, either.

When and if she returned.

Her aunts probably knew what had happened, why, and what to expect. They might even be able to tell her, now that the Tanya situation had been resolved. Regardless, Sabrina wasn't going to worry until she knew she had something to worry about.

Rising, Sabrina started back toward Too Chic Boutique. She was late, but she didn't look at her watch. After two days of being baited, blind-sided, and bullied, she needed a few more min-utes to unwind and adjust back to normal, even though normal in her life was bizarre by mortal standards.

She smiled, wondering if Cousin Jeffrey had turned himself into a horse when Aunt Hilda and Aunt Zelda had finally figured out spell shields. Since he had fathered Tanya, he obviously hadn't been a horse forever, but he had apparently learned to respect his peers and mortal asso-ciates.

Maybe Tanya would, too.

And maybe that's what this whole nightmare ordeal had been all about. Reviled, hunted, and persecuted in past centuries, witches had a lot of bad historical press to overcome. Any witch who didn't respect mortals and refused to keep a low profile posed a danger to all of her kind.

Keeping a low profile had definitely not been on Tanya's list of priorities, Sabrina observed as she wandered back down the concourse. Vendors and maintenance people were going about the business of cleaning up the evidence of Tanya's destructive rampage, with stoic determination. Catching snatches of conversation here and there, Sabrina was relieved to learn that several possible explanations for the seemingly inexplicable incidents of random devastation were being considered. Everything from an electromagnetic pulse, to the undetected shifting of tectonic plates, to the close passage of a renegade asteroid was being bandied about with varying degrees of credence.

No one proposed that a spoiled brat of a witch might have thrown a catastrophic temper tantrum.

Or that there might be lingering, delayed effects!

Sabrina stopped short as she passed the open doors into Toy Town. A huge pyramid of Green Slime cans in the center aisle was on the verge of collapsing. She raised her finger to stabilize the display, then quickly dropped it when a laughing child darted out from behind the stacked cans. The boy paused, then pulled a can out from the bottom. With a sharp intake of breath, Sabrina watched as the display crumbled, revealing Libby standing on the far side.

Arms and hands fumbling in a futile effort, Libby tried to prevent the clattering crash that sent slime cans rolling in all directions. Numb with failure and frustration, the cheerleader stared at the mess for several seconds, then slowly sank to her knees in the middle of the pile. When another child raised a glow-in-the-dark yellow launcher and let fly with a barrage of

Ping-Pong balls, Libby's only response to being hit repeatedly with the harmless but annoying plastic projectiles was to sigh in total despair.

Sabrina left before the cheerleader noticed her. She really wasn't in the mood to deal with another misguided vendetta just yet.

"Get 'em while they last!" The photo T-shirt vendor stood by his dented kiosk, waving a broken cup. "Don't miss this once-in-a-lifetime opportunity!"

"What opportunity?" a woman paused to ask. "Everything's broken."

"Exactly!" The man eyed her levelly. "How often do you get a chance to own something that was broken in an alien attack from outer space?"

"Aliens!" The woman gasped and glanced at the demolished kiosks around her. "Really? Is that what caused all this?"

"We'll probably never know." Lowering his voice, the man glanced furtively from side to side and tapped the broken cup. "But I wouldn't be surprised if this cup shows up on *Sightings* one of these days."

Sabrina grinned, amazed and impressed at how resourceful people could be under trying circumstances. *And how gullible,* she thought as the woman paid twice the original price for the broken cup.

"Hey, Sabrina!"

"Harvey!" Beaming, Sabrina hurried over to The Sports Palace, where Harvey was making sure none of the gathering onlookers got too close to the shattered glass and creaking metal beams dangling from the entrance overhang. A team of local firemen was inspecting the kiosk wedged in the doorway. "What happened here?" she asked innocently.

"Beats me." Shrugging, Harvey shook his head. "One minute I was arranging football jerseys by size on a rack and the next thing I know, this thing is charging toward me at a hundred miles an hour."

"Are you all right?" Sabrina faked a look of surprised concern.

"Yeah. It got stuck in the door. Funniest thing I ever saw." Waving a curious ten-year-old back, Harvey chuckled. "Now they're trying to figure out if they can pull it free without the roof caving in or something."

"Well, I'm glad you're okay."

"Thanks. I'm fine." Harvey nodded, his expression sobering. "Except for one thing. I really don't want to go to the movies with your cousin. No offense, but she gives me the creeps."

"No problem!" Sabrina couldn't help feeling a twinge of smug satisfaction at Harvey's honest revelation. "And don't worry about going to the movies with Tanya. She, uh—had to leave town—unexpectedly."

"Great!" Harvey grinned, then cleared his throat. "I mean, that's too bad."

"Yes," Sabrina agreed solemnly. "It is."

"But I'd rather go with you. *The Malibu Marauder* is playing again at five-thirty. Why don't you meet me at the Food Court when you get off?"

Sabrina gaped at him. "You're going to wait for me at the Food Court for *two* hours?"

"Sure. You're worth waiting for." Harvey shrugged again. "Besides, all this excitement has really made me hungry."

Shaking her head, Sabrina checked the time. One-twenty! Aubrey was going to have a fit! "I gotta run. See you at five!"

Dashing the rest of the way, Sabrina almost collided with Mr. Pool just outside Too Chic Boutique.

"Hey, Sabrina!" Turning away from the flooded plaza, Mr. Pool smiled down at her, then frowned slightly. "What's the hurry? You're not late getting back from lunch, are you?"

"Me? No way! We were busy earlier, so I went to lunch late. That's why I was running now. Just in case it got busy again." Sabrina shrugged.

"Good for you. I just stopped by to see how everyone was doing." Mr. Pool held up a hand to qualify his remark. "Not that I'm checking up on you guys or anything."

"No, of course not."

"Although I really was hoping to get some help in my yard this weekend." Mr. Pool sighed, then started as he looked past her down the concourse and saw the overturned, stuck, and demolished kiosks. Scratching his head, he glanced back at the fountain, which was swarming with bewildered maintenance men who were scratching their heads because they couldn't find anything wrong with the mechanism. "What happened, anyway? It looks like a tornado hit this place."

"Something like that." Sabrina nodded. *Tornado Tanya.*

"Well, you'd better get back to work. I'm gonna check this out." Mr. Pool started to walk away, then looked back. "Was anybody hurt?"

"No. Hard to believe, huh?"

"This is *all* hard to believe!"

Exhaling, Sabrina hesitated to look inside the store. Everything appeared to be under control, just as it had when she had flown by a short time ago.

Except for Aubrey.

The manager's smile was strained and she swayed slightly as she scanned another price into the register. Wisps of flyaway red hair drifted across a forehead furrowed with exhaustion, and she looked curiously shorter. Sabrina hurried inside before the poor woman wilted entirely.

With a quick flick of her hand, Sabrina reset Aubrey's watch and all the clocks in the store. She couldn't reverse time, but nothing prevented her from setting timepieces back twenty minutes. She'd just slowly adjust them forward again as the afternoon progressed.

"I'm back!"

"Finally!" Handing a customer her bagged purchases, Aubrey looked at the long line of people still waiting, and sighed with dismay. "Excuse me for a moment . . ."

"Sure." The next customer in line picked up a scarf and stared at it thoughtfully for a moment before she placed it on the counter.

Rubbing her temples, Aubrey staggered to a nearby chair in her stockinged feet. The platform shoes were stuffed in the wastebasket behind the counter, which accounted for her dramatic decrease in height. "You're late."

"I don't think so." Frowning with feigned worry, Sabrina checked her watch. "No, it's just past one."

"Really? Seems like you've been gone for hours." Sprawling in the chair, Aubrey blew the stray wisps of hair off her face. "But I'm glad you're back. The cash register's all yours. I need a break."

"Okay!" As Sabrina started to turn, Aubrey called her back.

The manager was grinning despite her weariness. "We've already broken the Saturday sales record, Sabrina. If this keeps up, we'll set a record no one will ever be able to top!" Raising a victorious fist, she winked, then slumped and closed her eyes. "Wake me when it's over."

"Right!" The sight that met Sabrina's gaze as she turned toward the counter dampened her eagerness a bit.

Twenty women and girls stood in line. Several others roamed the aisles, arms laden with sweaters, skirts, slacks, and shirts. Since no one was in a hurry, Sabrina made a quick circuit of the store. She wisely decided to let the patience spell stand until the rush had run its course, but one by one she transformed the enchanted mirrors back to normal. The sales record had already been broken and Aubrey was guaranteed a new record that would be impossible to break. Besides, when five o'clock came, Sabrina didn't want anything or anyone to keep her from meeting Harvey.

Smiling with genuine enthusiasm, Sabrina dashed behind the counter. Picking up the scarf on top of the customer's pile, she ran the scanner over the price tag and glanced at the register.

A bell chimed and the digital symbols on the register's readout whirled, stopped, then flashed in glowing orange.

Sabrina laughed. The conflict with Tanya *had* been a test, just as she suspected. Exactly *what* she had been tested for didn't seem important right now, though. The grades were in.

PASS!

About the Author

Diana G. Gallagher lives in Minnesota with her husband, Marty Burke, three dogs, three cats, and a cranky parrot. When she's not writing, she likes to read, walk the dogs, and look for cool stuff at garage sales for her grandsons, Jonathan, Alan, and Joseph.

Diana and Marty are musicians who perform traditional and original Irish and American folk music at coffeehouses and conventions around the country. Marty sings and plays the twelve-string guitar and banjo. In addition to singing backup harmonies, Diana plays rhythm guitar and a round Celtic drum called a *bodhran*.

A Hugo Award–winning artist, Diana is best known for her series *Woof: The House Dragon*. Her first adult novel, *The Alien Dark*, appeared in 1990. She and Marty coauthored *The Chance Factor*, a *Starfleet Academy Voyager* book. In addition to other *Star Trek* novels for intermediate readers, Diana has written many books in other series published by Minstrel Books, including *The Secret World of Alex Mack, Are You Afraid of the Dark?* and *The Mystery Files of Shelby Woo*. She is currently working on her next book.

You love the TV show, now you can read the books!

moesha

A brand-new book series coming in September 1997

#1 Everybody Say Moesha!

Can Mo keep her love classified?

01147-2/$3.99

#2 Keeping It Real

Mo's boyfriend's got it going on.
But has he got something going on the side?

01148-0/$3.99

Available from Archway Paperbacks
Published by Pocket Books

Sometimes, it takes a kid to solve a good crime...

THE MYSTERY FILES of SHELBY WOO™

Original stories based on the hit Nickelodeon show!

#1 A Slash in the Night
by Alan Goodman

#2 Takeout Stakeout
By Diana G. Gallagher
(Coming in mid-June 1997)

#3 Rock 'n' Roll Robbery
by Lydia C. Marano and David Cody Weiss
(Coming in mid-August 1997)

#4 Hot Rock
by John Peel
(Coming in mid-October 1997)

To find out more about *The Mystery Files of Shelby Woo* or any other Nickelodeon show, visit Nickelodeon Online on America Online (Keyword: NICK) or send e-mail (NickMailDD@aol.com).

A MINSTREL BOOK
Published by Pocket Books

1352